AXIOM OF THE INDOMITABLE HUMAN SPIRIT

JOSIAS MIBZSTARUS

Published by Josias Mibzstarus
Author: Josias Mibzstarus
Email: Axiomseries14@gmail.com

ISBN: 978-1-969458-00-2 https://amazon.com/author/josias
https://www.amazon.com/dp/B0DDRHXWN5

Author's Thoughts

It is my honor to write my thoughts into a story that people all around the world might understand and appreciate it, enjoying a work I hope to continue expanding on in a universe open for exploration by the story's end. This first book came about in one of the loneliest and scariest times in my life, one I hope never to relive again. These are my thoughts turned to paper so that I may continue fighting the good fight, not only surviving as a child but living through it so I may live as an adult. My hopes are for readers to immerse themselves in this chaotic world, investing their emotions on the human connection so we may all one day ascend to a better place, planting our human light across the world to the universe and beyond. There are many more stories to tell within this universe. This is only the beginning.

ENJOY!

Josias Mibzstarus, from the Isle of Mibzstar

AXIOM
AXIOM: OF THE
INDOMITABLE HUMAN SPIRIT

Contents

5 Table of Contents

6 Emergence

55 Defiance

88 Clash Between Hope and Despair

139 Arrival of Hope

CHAPTER ONE:
THE
EMERGENCE

Emergence

As the time struck three o'clock on the ninth of that fateful July afternoon in 2016, an eerie darkness descended upon the world. It was no ordinary twilight; this darkness bore hues of red, orange, and yellow, tinged with a menacing blackness. Confusion rippled through the air as people exchanged bewildered glances, their routines shattered by the unexpected phenomenon.

"The weatherman didn't mention an eclipse today," muttered a man, voicing the collective disbelief.

But before anyone could grasp the full extent of the strangeness unfolding, the ground beneath them began to tremble. Panic seized the hearts of the populace as they fled in all directions, fearing an earthquake. Yet it was not the earth's shifting plates that heralded calamity.

With a malevolent grace, the soil split apart, revealing a sinister portal which defied the very laws of nature. From within this ominous tear in the ground a searing blaze erupted, its fiery tendrils reaching skyward, almost piercing the heavens themselves. It was a sight that struck terror into the hearts of all who beheld it, a portent of dark forces stirring from their slumber.

As darkness enveloped the world and the ground trembled beneath their feet, fear and confusion gripped the hearts of the people, for they had never witnessed such an ominous event. The sudden appearance of the portal, spewing forth flames of an otherworldly nature, seemed to herald a cataclysmic event beyond their comprehension. In the face of such a terrifying spectacle, the fate of humanity hung precariously in the balance as they grappled with the unknown forces that had been unleashed upon their world.

As the planet trembled and the roar echoed across the world, anticipation and dread mingled in the hearts of those who remained. The flaming gout from the depths unveiled a colossal shadow in the form of a dragon, igniting both fear and fascination among the onlookers. But as the flames subsided, what emerged was not the majestic creature of legend but a grotesque being, alien and malevolent in its

Emergence

appearance. Its presence sent shivers down the spines of those who beheld it, for it was clear this creature was not of heavenly origin but a harbinger of darkness and despair.

As the dragon, forged by Lucifer himself, descended upon the earth with its seven heads and fearsome form, chaos and devastation ensued. Its landing unleashed a torrent of flames, transforming the once-vibrant planet into a barren wasteland reminiscent of the desolate surface of the moon.

Despite the dwindling numbers of survivors, their prayers for salvation went unanswered; the wrath of evil seemed insurmountable. In the face of such overwhelming darkness, the hope for divine intervention waned, leaving humanity to endure the torment inflicted upon them by the monstrous dragon and its master. Amidst the destruction wrought by the dragon called Babylon, the remaining survivors sought refuge deep underground, in the dark recesses of the sewers. Here they faced starvation and despair, clinging to the last shreds of their humanity as they struggled to endure. Yet, even in the depths of darkness, a glimmer of hope flickered within their hearts.

As one woman voiced her doubts and fears, questioning the absence of divine intervention, an elder offered solace and reassurance. He urged her to hold fast to her faith, to trust in the promise of a higher power who would come in their darkest hour. In his embrace, she found comfort and renewed determination, vowing to believe not only in the face of adversity but beyond it, for faith transcends even the darkest of nights.

The whispered words of defiance echoed through the underground sanctuary, stirring a sense of determination among the survivors. For a large number, the idea of relying solely on their own strength and courage resonated deeply, casting aside the notion of waiting passively for divine intervention. In the face of overwhelming darkness, the call to action sparked a flicker of hope, empowering them to rise from the depths of fear and uncertainty.

Emergence

With each passing moment, the resolve to confront the
dragon and its master grew stronger, fueled by the belief that
they possessed the capacity to fight for their survival.
While faith in a higher power provided solace to some, others
found courage in the conviction that they could forge their
own destiny, even in the face of chaos and despair.
United by their shared determination, they prepared to
emerge from the shadows, ready to confront the darkness that
threatened to consume them.
The choice of America as the site for Lucifer's throne
reflected Babylon's understanding of human resilience and
the spirit of defiance that resonated deeply within the nation.
Aware of America's history of fighting for freedom and
standing against tyranny, Babylon saw it as a strategic
location to assert his dominance and crush any remaining
resistance.
However, despite the devastation wrought upon the earth and
the overwhelming power of Babylon and his minions, there
remained a glimmer of hope in the indomitable spirit of
humanity. The prospect of resistance, of fighting back against
the darkness that threatened to engulf them had not been lost
on those who refused to surrender to despair.

***

As Babylon rallies his warriors to fulfill his master's bidding,
the stage is set for a battle of epic proportions, where the fate
of humanity hangs in the balance. Though the odds may seem
insurmountable, the flame of hope burns bright in the hearts
of those who dare to defy the darkness, holding onto the
belief that even in the darkest hour, the light of courage and
resilience will prevail.
The interdimensional portal in the bleeding clouds disgorges
millions of warrior demons, the sky becoming a swirling
maelstrom of darkness and malevolence. Babylon, his
colossal wings outstretched, proclaims their arrival to the

world, heralding the beginning of an era of darkness and despair.

The word "HELL" reverberates across the globe, striking fear into the hearts of all who hear it, for it signifies the reign of darkness and the triumph of evil. As the demon horde gathers under Babylon's command, the earth trembles beneath their collective might and the last vestiges of hope seem to fade away.

Yet, even in the face of such overwhelming darkness, there are those who refuse to yield, who cling to the belief that light will triumph over darkness. As the forces of Hell gather for their final assault, the stage is set for a battle that will determine the fate of humanity itself.

In the dimly lit underground tunnels of New York City, the chilling echoes of the word "hell" reverberate through the air, sending shivers down the spines of all who hear it. Fear grips the hearts of the people, their sense of helplessness amplified by the overwhelming darkness surrounding them.

Amidst the uncertainty and despair, a glimmer of determination flickers in the eyes of many, a spark of resilience amidst the darkness. Though they may feel powerless in the face of such unfathomable evil, they refuse to succumb to despair. Instead, they cling to the hope that, together, they can find a way to fight back against the forces of darkness that threaten to consume them.

In the depths of the underground labyrinth, whispers of defiance begin to spread as the survivors gather, united by their shared resolve to resist the darkness encroaching on their world. Though the path ahead may be fraught with peril, they know they cannot surrender to fear. For in the darkest of times, it is their courage and determination that will light the way forward.

As the demon warriors spread across the world, conducting Babylon's command to bring all remaining people to the throne of Lucifer, fear and despair grip those who find themselves targeted by their relentless pursuit. From every corner of the earth, people are hunted down and herded toward the designated location, compelled to recognize their new master, and submit to his will.

Meanwhile, in the underground tunnels beneath New York City, Babylon and his chosen warriors prepare to receive the captured survivors. With a display of formidable strength, Babylon carves a path through the earth, creating a massive crater into which the demons and their prisoners descend.

As Babylon approaches the gathered people, their defiance is met with overwhelming force, leaving them powerless to resist. Despite their attempts to fight back, they are no match for the superior strength and malevolent power of the demon horde.

With each captive brought before the throne of Lucifer, the darkness tightens its grip on the world, the reign of evil reaching its zenith. Yet, amidst the despair and suffering, a flicker of hope remains, for even in the darkest of times the human spirit endures, resilient and unwavering in its quest for freedom and redemption.

In the face of such overwhelming darkness and tyranny, the beleaguered survivors keenly feel the absence of a savior.

As they await the arrival of Babylon and his master Lucifer, the desperation and despair in their hearts weigh heavily upon them.

When Babylon returns to the throne of his master, ready to compel the people to bow down before Lucifer, a lone voice rises from the crowd, defiant and unyielding. But before the words of resistance can fully take hold, Babylon's swift and merciless response silences the dissent, leaving nothing but ashes in its wake.

Amid such cruelty and oppression, the question of where their savior is remains unanswered. With each act of violence and domination, the hope for deliverance diminishes, leaving the people to face their darkest hour alone.

Yet, even in the face of such overwhelming evil, the flame of resistance still burns within the hearts of humankind.

Emergence

Though their voices may be quenched their spirits remain unbroken, ready to defy the darkness and fight for freedom until their last breath.

As the corruption continues to envelop the world and the weight of despair presses down upon the hearts of the people, a sense of resignation settles over them. Babylon's proclamation of their fate as slaves or warriors for hell leaves them with no choice but to acquiesce, their spirits drained by the relentless onslaught of evil.

With each passing day, the memory of a world bathed in light fades further into obscurity, replaced by the bleak reality of their existence under the dominion of darkness.

Hope, once a beacon of resilience, now lies dormant within them, overshadowed by the oppressive despair that grips their souls.

Yet, amidst the desolation and suffering, a glimmer of defiance still flickers within the heart of Earth's descendants. They remember a time when standing up for what they believed in was worth more than their own lives, when the bonds of humanity transcended the darkness now threatening to consume them.

As they tread the path of uncertainty and despair, they cling to the belief that suffering is not the way that there must be a glimmer of light amidst the darkness, a spark of hope that will one day ignite the flames of resistance and redemption. Though the road ahead may be fraught with peril, they refuse to surrender to despair, for they know that even in the darkest of times, the human spirit has the power to endure and overcome.

***

Amidst the darkness and despair that has gripped the world, there are still pockets of resistance, hidden away and biding their time for the right moment to act. These are the individuals who have spent their lives preparing for the possibility of such a cataclysmic event, honing their skills and gathering resources to protect their loved ones and their country.

In upstate New York and the Hudson Valley area, two families with deep military roots and connections to various governments and black sites have taken refuge underground, communicating through CB radios and coordinating their efforts to resist the encroaching forces of darkness.

With their expertise in military tactics and advanced technology, these families are poised to lead the charge against the tyranny of Babylon and Lucifer, harnessing their knowledge and resources to wage a war for the survival of humanity.

Their determination and resilience serve as a beacon of hope for those who still dare to believe that light can triumph over darkness. As they emerge from the shadows and into the fray, they carry with them the promise of a new dawn, where humanity can once again rise from the ashes and reclaim its place in the light.

As the families from upstate New York make their way to Stewart Airport, they traverse through a landscape of devastation and death, where the stench of decay hangs heavy in the air and the flames of destruction cast an eerie glow upon the desolate surroundings. Despite the horrors they encounter along the way, they press on, fueled by their unwavering determination to confront the darkness threatening to consume their world.

Arriving at the airport, they find themselves prepared for a fight, expecting resistance from the demons that lurk in the shadows. However, to their surprise, there is no immediate confrontation, only an unsettling silence that hangs over the deserted airport.

They prepare to rendezvous with the other family, steeling themselves for the battle that lies ahead, knowing that their sacrifice may be the only hope for humanity's survival. With their hearts filled with courage and resolve, they stand ready to face the demons and their master, Lucifer, with the determination to fight until their last breath.

Emergence

As the family's military Humvee rolls down the road toward Stewart Airport, tension fills the air as they remain vigilant, weapons at the ready, scanning their surroundings for any sign of danger. When one of the sons alerts the father to a potential threat, a moment of uncertainty passes before the father reassures him, attributing the movement to natural causes or surviving wildlife.

However, as the jeep comes to a sudden stop and the atmosphere grows tense, the family springs into action, assigning positions to each member with practiced efficiency. James takes point at the front, Biggs secures the rear, and Josias positions himself atop the jeep, scanning for any signs of danger. Eli, the three men's father, as well as their friends Adonis and Ethan stand ready to defend the Humvee, their determination unwavering in the face of the looming threat. With their eyes fixed on the horizon and their hearts set on reclaiming their world from the clutches of Babylon, the family moves forward with a steely resolve, ready to confront whatever challenges lie ahead in their mission to restore humanity's hope and freedom.

As the tense confrontation with the demon knights unfolds, the family finds themselves locked in a desperate struggle for survival. Despite their formidable weaponry, the demon knights prove to be powerful adversaries, with supernatural strength and agility that far surpasses that of mere mortals. When Josias finds himself in a perilous situation, facing down a demon knight intent on snapping his neck, he refuses to succumb to fear. With quick thinking and sheer determination, he manages to turn the tables, using the demon knight's own momentum against it and gaining the upper hand.

As the battle rages on, Josias unleashes a flurry of bullets upon his demonic assailant, finally managing to bring him down with a well-placed shot to the head. But with five more demon knights still standing, the fight is far from over, and the odds remain stacked against them.

Emergence

With adrenaline coursing through his veins and determination burning bright in his eyes, Josias braces himself for the next onslaught, knowing that the fate of humanity hangs in the balance. With every fiber of his being, he is prepared to fight to the end, for the honor of his family, his people, and his world.

As Josias rushes to assist his brother James in the heat of battle, the chaos and intensity of the confrontation reach new heights. James finds himself locked in combat with a demon knight, struggling to gain the upper hand as the creature bears down on him with ferocious intent.

Determination burning bright in his eyes, James refuses to back down, unleashing a barrage of gunfire that tears through the demon knight's form, reducing it to two separate pieces. As he celebrates his victory, he quickly turns his attention to his friend Adonis, who is in dire need of assistance.

Rushing to Adonis's aid, James tackles the demon knight threatening his friend with the force of a charging linebacker, freeing Adonis from the creature's grasp. As they catch their breath, the demon knight rises once more, its wings flapping with menacing intent as it taunts them with threats of impending doom.

Despite the demon knight's ominous warnings, Adonis and James refuse to surrender to fear, their determination to fight back against the forces of darkness burning stronger than ever. With a defiant retort and a steely resolve, they prepare to face whatever challenges lie ahead, knowing the fate of humanity hangs in the balance.

As the demon knight closes in for the kill, Adonis and James share a moment of camaraderie, their spirits unbroken even in the face of overwhelming odds. With Adonis watching from a distance, their resolve is unwavering, their determination to defy the darkness stronger than ever before. The intense battle reaches its climax, the family members fighting with everything they have, determined to rid their world of the demonic threat for the last time. Adonis's quick thinking and daring maneuver save James from a deadly fall, and together they use the demon knight's own momentum to defeat it, crashing the creature into another demon knight and bringing both to their end.

Meanwhile, Biggs unleashes a barrage of gunfire upon the demon he is battling, refusing to relent until the creature lies defeated at his feet. With adrenaline coursing through their veins and anger driving their actions, the family fights with a ferocity born of desperation and determination.

As they regroup the absence of their father is deeply felt, but their relief is palpable when he emerges from the darkness, dragging the body of the last demon knight behind him. His words ring with defiance and resolve, reminding his sons and their companions that despite their otherworldly abilities, the demons are mortal creatures who must be defeated.

With renewed determination and unity, the family stands together, ready to face whatever challenges lie ahead in their quest to reclaim their world from the clutches of darkness. For in their hearts burns the flame of hope, and in their hands lies the power to shape their own destiny.

As the family takes control of Stewart Airport, Josias's words serve as a rallying cry, igniting their determination to confront Babylon and his demonic followers head-on. With their weapons reloaded and their resolve hardened, they ride toward their destination with a singular focus: to rid the world of the consuming gloom.

***

Meanwhile, in New York City, Babylon senses the approaching threat of the family, his fury echoing across the planet as a warning to all who dare to oppose him. Yet, far from being deterred by his menacing roar, the family remains steadfast in their mission, refusing to be intimidated by the evil that surrounds them. With Eli's leadership guiding them, the family presses on, their hearts filled with the fierce determination to reclaim their world and restore humanity's rightful place in the sun.

Emergence

They prepare to face the ultimate battle against Babylon and his minions, drawing strength from their unity and their unwavering belief in the righteousness of their cause.

With each passing moment, the tension mounts, and the fate of the world hangs in the balance. But as they stand on the precipice of destiny, the family knows they are not alone in their fight. Together, they will face whatever challenges lie ahead, united in their resolve to reclaim their humanity and bring an end to the reign of darkness that threatens to engulf them all.

As Josias communicates with their friends in Pennsylvania, he reassures them that they have the capability to combat the demon-like creatures they encounter. Despite encountering a barricade, Josias encourages Mike to remain calm, emphasizing that the demonic entities can be harmed by human weapons.

With a plan to regroup at Stewart Airport and face their adversaries together, Josias assures Mike that they will see each other soon and wishes them luck as they navigate the obstacles in their path.

Determination fills their hearts and solidarity swells among their ranks, the families and their allies remaining resolute in their mission to confront the forces of darkness and reclaim their world from the grip of evil.

Mike's words are ringing in their ears as the group prepares to face the demonic threat head-on. Gage's remark adds a touch of dark humor to the tense situation, lightening the mood momentarily as they gear up for battle.

As they load their weapons and prepare for the confrontation ahead, each member of the group is brimming with a steely determination to fight until they are victorious. With their resolve strengthened by their unity and shared purpose, they stand ready to confront the forces of darkness and protect humanity from encroaching evil.

With their sights set on victory, they steel themselves for the battle ahead, knowing that the fate of the world hangs in the balance. United in their determination and armed with their unwavering resolve, they prepare to face whatever challenges lie ahead, ready to stand as the last line of defense against the growing darkness.

As Gage unleashes a barrage of grenades toward the demon knights, the explosion creates a temporary reprieve from the onslaught of fiery energy beams. With the immediate threat neutralized, Mike urges Gage to return to the safety of the armored vehicle so they can regroup and continue their journey.

However, as Gage prepares to re-enter the vehicle, a furious growl pierces the air, freezing him in place. It is a chilling reminder that their battle is far from over, and the demons will stop at nothing to destroy them. With tension mounting and uncertainty looming, the group braces themselves for the next phase of the conflict, knowing they must remain vigilant and united to survive the relentless assault of the demonic forces.

With the fate of humanity hanging in the balance, they steel themselves for the challenges that lie ahead, determined to emerge victorious against the forces of darkness. As Gage finds himself at the mercy of the demon knight, his heart pounds with a mixture of fear and defiance. Despite the dire situation, he refuses to cower before the creature, his eyes flashing with determination.

Summoning every ounce of courage, Gage stares bravely into the demon knight's eyes and retorts, "I'll never beg for mercy from the likes of you. Do you think you can scare us into submission? You're nothing but a pathetic pawn of darkness."

With fierce determination burning within him, Gage braces himself for whatever fate may come, knowing he will face it with unwavering resolve. As the demon knight prepares to unleash its wrath upon him, Gage remains steadfast, ready to confront his destiny head-on and prove that, even in the face of overwhelming evil, the indomitable human spirit will never be extinguished.

Emergence

As the demon knight falls to the ground, defeated by the relentless barrage of gunfire, a sense of relief washes over Mike, Hunter, Charlie, and Gage. Despite their exhaustion and wounds they stand victorious over their fallen adversary, knowing they have prevailed against the evil.

Gage, still reeling from his encounter with the demon knight, struggles to catch his breath as he surveys the scene before him. Despite the pain and fatigue, a sense of triumph fills his heart as he realizes they have overcome yet another obstacle in their quest to reclaim their world from the clutches of wickedness.

With the immediate threat neutralized, Mike, Hunter, Charlie, and Gage gather their wits and prepare to continue their journey toward Stewart Airport. Though they know that more challenges lie ahead, they are undeterred, determined to confront whatever may come their way.

They set out once more their resolve stronger than ever, fueled by the knowledge that they are fighting not just for their own survival, but for the future of all humanity. With each step forward, they draw closer to their goal: to defeat the darkness and restore light to their shattered world.

As they speed through the Wallkill area of New York, Mike, Gage, and their cousins encounter a swarm of demon knights blocking their path, determined to halt their progress. With no time to waste, they brace themselves for another confrontation, knowing they must fight their way through if they are to reach Stewart Airport and join forces with their friends.

Mike steers the armored tank with precision, weaving through the chaotic scene as demon knights swarm around them, unleashing blasts of energy and fury. Gage, Hunter, and Charlie stand ready at their positions, armed to the teeth, their weapons loaded with armor-piercing ammunition.

As the demon knights close in, Mike orders his comrades to open fire, unleashing a barrage of bullets and grenades upon their adversaries. The air fills with the deafening roar of gunfire and the acrid smell of burning flesh as the demon knights are torn apart by the onslaught.

Despite the ferocity of their attackers, Mike, Gage, Hunter, and Charlie stand their ground, their determination unyielding as they push forward through the chaos. With each demon knight that falls they draw closer to their goal, their resolve stronger than ever.

As they continue their relentless advance, they know their journey is far from over. But with courage and determination as their guiding lights, they press on, ready to face whatever challenges lie ahead in their quest to confront the dragon called Babylon and reclaim their world from the forces of darkness.

As they steel themselves for the battle ahead, Mike, Gage, Hunter, and Charlie draw upon their inner strength and determination, refusing to back down in the face of overwhelming odds. Despite the chaos and fear surrounding them, they cling to the hope that they can make a difference, even if it means sacrificing everything.

With Hunter's words of encouragement ringing in their ears, they focus their attention on the task at hand, ready to confront the demon knights with everything they have.

Mike takes the lead, issuing orders to his comrades and directing their movements with precision and determination. As they engage the demon knights in combat, they fight with a fierce resolve, unleashing a relentless onslaught of firepower upon their adversaries. Each demon knight that falls fuels their determination to press on, knowing their fight is not in vain.

Despite the odds stacked against them, they refuse to give up, knowing that their actions could mean the difference between victory and defeat for humanity. With every moment that passes, they draw closer to their goal, their spirits undaunted by the darkness that surrounds them.

Together, they stand as a beacon of hope in the face of despair, ready to fight until their last breath if it means protecting their world and their loved ones from the forces of evil. As they continue to battle against the demon knights they know their resolve will be refined like never before, but they are determined to emerge victorious, no matter the cost. With their friend Josias on the way, Mike, Gage, Hunter, and Charlie steel themselves for the imminent battle against the demon knights. They know their survival depends on holding off the demons until reinforcements arrive, and they are determined to fight with all their strength.

As they prepare for the onslaught, they check their weapons, ensuring they are fully loaded and ready for action. Each of them takes a moment to center themselves, drawing upon their inner strength and resolve to face the coming challenge head-on.

With the countdown to Josias' arrival ticking away, they assume defensive positions, ready to repel the demons with a relentless barrage of firepower. Despite the fear and uncertainty gripping them, they remain steadfast in their determination to protect each other and push back against the forces of evil.

As the first wave of demon knights descends upon them, they unleash a torrent of bullets and grenades, fighting with a ferocity born of desperation and defiance. Each demon that falls only serves to fuel their determination, driving them to fight harder and hold the line against overwhelming odds. With every passing moment, they draw closer to their goal, knowing their friends are on their way to join the fight. As they continue to battle against the demon knights, they cling to the hope that they will emerge victorious and live to fight another day.

***

With a sense of urgency and determination, Eli and his family load up their jeep with the strongest weapons they have, preparing for another intense battle against the demon knights. They know that time is of the essence and that they must act quickly to save their friends trapped in Wallkill.

Emergence

As they gear up for battle, each member of the family steels themselves for the fight ahead, drawing upon their courage and resolve. They know that the odds are stacked against them, but they refuse to back down in the face of adversity. With their weapons loaded and their hearts set on saving their friends, Eli and his family set out toward Wallkill, determined to show the demon knights they are not to be underestimated. They drive with a sense of purpose, knowing that the lives of their friends hang in the balance and that they are their only hope for survival.

As they approach the battlefield, they see the demon knights closing in on their friends, unleashing a barrage of attacks. Without hesitation, Eli and his family charged into the fray, guns blazing, ready to take on the forces of evil and rescue their comrades.

With every shot fired and every demon knight defeated, they draw closer to their friends, fighting with all their strength and determination. They know that the fate of their companions' rests in their hands, and they refuse to let them down.

As the battle rages on, Eli and his family fight side by side, pushing back against the demon knights with unwavering resolve. With each passing moment, they come closer to victory, knowing that their bravery and sacrifice will not be in vain.

Finally, after what feels like an eternity, they emerge victoriously, having defeated the demon knights and saved their friends from certain doom. As they stand amidst the wreckage of the battlefield, they share a moment of relief and triumph, knowing that they have proven themselves to be true warriors in the face of darkness. As the battle intensifies, Mike and his family fight valiantly against the demon knights, unleashing a bombardment of gunfire in an attempt to hold them off until their friends arrive. With each shot fired, they inch closer to victory, determined to eliminate the threat posed by the demon Knights more sooner than later.

Emergence

***

Despite the overwhelming odds, Mike and his family refuse to back down, standing their ground against the relentless onslaught of their demonic foes. With every bullet that finds its mark, they chip away at the enemy's numbers, determined to prevail against all odds.

As the battle rages on, they fight with a ferocity born of desperation, knowing the fate of not only themselves but also their friends and the world itself hangs in the balance. Each moment feels like an eternity as they struggle to keep the demon knights at bay, their resolve unwavering in the face of adversity.

But even as they fight, they can sense that the tide of battle is turning against them. The demon knights, fueled by their unholy rage, seem inexhaustible, pressing forward with an unrelenting fury that threatens to overwhelm them at any moment.

The odds are still against Mike and his family, but they refuse to give up hope, knowing their friends from upstate New York are on their way to lend assistance. With their determination and undiminished courage, they continue to fight, holding out for the moment when reinforcements will arrive to turn the tide of battle in their favor.

With their ammunition depleted and the demon knights closing in, Mike and his family find themselves facing an imminent threat. Despite the odds stacked against them, Mike refuses to surrender, instead choosing to confront the demon knights head-on with nothing but his bare hands.

With a defiant shout, Mike challenges the demon knights to face him in hand-to-hand combat, ready to unleash his fury on them with every ounce of strength he possesses. As the demon knights charge toward him, Mike stands his ground, his fists clenched, eyes filled with determination.

With each blow he lands, Mike strikes fear into the hearts of the demon knights, showing them that he will not go down without a fight. Despite their supernatural abilities, the

Emergence

demon knights find themselves struggling to keep up with Mike's relentless assault, their once-vaunted powers proving no match for his sheer willpower and determination.

As the battle rages , Mike fights with a ferocity born of desperation, knowing that the fate of his family and friends hangs in the balance. With every punch he throws, he inches closer to victory, refusing to back down, even in the face of overwhelming odds.

And then, just when it seems like all hope has been lost, a familiar sound echoes in the distance. The roar of engines and the rumble of heavy machinery signal the arrival of Eli and his family, their reinforcements finally arriving to hopefully turn the tide of battle in their favor.

As Mike lies on the ground, battered and broken, his body wracked with pain, he gazes into the darkness, his spirit fading as the realization dawns upon him that their battle may have reached its end. The demonic assailants surround them, their malevolent presence looming over Mike and his family like a dark cloud.

In his darkest hour, Mike's thoughts turn to his loved ones, his brother and cousins who fought bravely by his side until the very end. Despite their best efforts, they find themselves overwhelmed by the sheer number and ferocity of their enemies, their bodies battered and bruised, their strength waning with each passing moment.

As the darkness closes in around them, Mike's mind drifts to the possibility of death, the inevitable end that now looms ever closer. But even in the face of despair, he finds a flicker of hope, a glimmer of light amidst the darkness.

Suddenly, a pair of shining eyes pierce through the gloom, illuminating the darkness with a faint glow. For a moment, Mike feels a surge of hope, a spark of defiance that refuses to be stamped out.

But as quickly as it appeared, the light fades, leaving Mike and his family once again engulfed in darkness. Yet, in that fleeting moment, Mike finds solace in the knowledge that even in the darkest of times there is still a glimmer of hope, a beacon of light that refuses to be smothered.

And so, as they face their inevitable fate, Mike and his family cling to that glimmer of hope, drawing strength from the knowledge that they fought bravely until the very end, their spirits unbroken, their courage undiminished. And though their journey may have reached its end, their legacy will live on, a testament to the indomitable human spirit and the power of hope in the face of darkness.

As the demon knights lunge forward, eager to engage in battle with Eli, James, Biggs, Josias, Adonis, and Ethan, they quickly realize they have underestimated their opponents. The air fills with the sound of gunfire and the clash of steel as the two sides engage in fierce combat.

Eli and his family fight with unwavering determination, their weapons flashing in the darkness as they stand firm against the onslaught of demon knights. Each blow is faced with equal force, each attack countered with skill and precision. Despite the odds stacked against them, Eli and his family refuse to back down, their resolve unshakable as they fight to defend their fallen comrades and protect the world from the forces of darkness.

With each passing moment, the tide of battle begins to turn in their favor. The demon knights, once confident in their superiority, now find themselves struggling to hold their ground against the relentless onslaught of Eli and his family. As the battle rages on, the demon knights are driven back, their ranks decimated by the fierce determination and unwavering courage of their human adversaries. And in the end, it is Eli and his family who emerge victorious, their triumph a testament to the indomitable spirit of humanity in the face of overwhelming darkness.

As Adonis's quick thinking saves him from the demon knight's grasp, Josias engages in a fierce hand-to-hand battle with another demon knight, dodging its strikes and delivering powerful blows of his own. With each punch and kick, Josias fights with all his might, determined to overcome his opponent and protect his family.

Meanwhile Eli and his sons—James along with Biggs— unleash a barrage of gunfire and explosives, driving back the demon knights and clearing a path for their allies. Their weapons blaze with fury as they mow down the demonic forces, their aims come true and resolve unwavering.

Despite the ferocity of the demon knights, Eli and his family stand firm, their courage shining brightly in the face of such evil. With each demon knight they defeat, they draw closer to victory, their determination fueling their relentless assault.

As the battle rages on, the demon knights find themselves overwhelmed by the sheer determination and strength of their human adversaries. With every demon knight that falls, Eli and his family grow stronger, their bond unbreakable as they fight side by side to protect their world from the forces of corruption.

As Josias struggles beneath the demon knight's grasp, his mind races with worry for his injured friends and family. Despite the pain and fear, he knows he must focus on the immediate threat before him. Summoning all his strength and determination, Josias fights against the demon knight with every ounce of his being, refusing to yield even in the face of overwhelming odds.

With a burst of adrenaline, Josias manages to break free from the demon knight's grip, staggering to his feet as he prepares to continue the fight. Despite the chaos and danger surrounding him, his thoughts are consumed by the need to protect his loved ones and defeat the demonic forces that threaten their lives.

With a fierce battle cry, Josias launches himself back into the fray, his fists flying as he strikes out against the demon knights with unmatched ferocity. Every blow he lands is ignited by his determination to emerge victorious and ensure the safety of those he holds dear. As he fights on, Josias knows he cannot afford to falter or hesitate. He must push himself to the limit and fight with all his heart: the fate of his friends, his family, and the world itself hangs in the balance. With unwavering resolve, he presses forward, ready to face whatever challenges lie ahead in his quest for victory.

Despite the searing pain in his shoulder, Josias pushes through, his focus unwavering as he rushes to his family's side. With each step his determination to protect them only grows stronger, driving him forward even in the face of his own injuries.

As he reaches his fallen loved ones, Josias checks on each of them, assessing their conditions and doing his best to tend to their wounds. With adrenaline coursing through his veins, he works quickly and efficiently, applying makeshift bandages and offering words of reassurance to his family members. Despite the chaos and danger surrounding them, Josias remains steadfast in his resolve to keep his family safe. With each passing moment, his determination burns brighter, fueling his efforts to protect those he holds dear from the relentless onslaught of the demonic forces.

Though his own injuries weigh heavily on him, Josias pushes through the pain, drawing strength from his love for his family and his unwavering commitment to their survival. As he fights to keep them safe, he knows he must remain vigilant and prepared to face whatever challenges lie ahead in their desperate struggle for survival.

As they drive toward Stewart Airport, the two families feel a mix of determination and apprehension. They know that their encounter with Babylon will be their greatest challenge yet, but they have resolved themselves to face it directly, united in their mission to rid the world of the demonic threat.

With each passing mile, their sense of urgency grows, spurred on by the knowledge that time is running out and Babylon's forces are gathering strength. They push their vehicles to their limits, driven by a fierce determination to reach their destination and confront their enemy before it is too late.

They finally arrive at Stewart Airport, and the families share a moment of respite, taking a moment to gather their strength and prepare themselves for the battle ahead. They know that they must remain focused and united if they are to stand any chance against Babylon and his minions.

With their weapons at the ready and their resolve steeled, the families set out toward their final confrontation with Babylon, knowing the fate of humanity hangs in the balance. As they face the darkness ahead, they draw strength from each other, ready to fight to the end to protect their world and those they love.

As they prepare their fleet and military artillery, the tension among the group is palpable. They know that the time for action is drawing near. Despite their exhaustion and the uncertainty of what lies ahead, they are resolute in their determination to confront Babylon and his forces head-on. They finalize their plans and make preparations, sparing a moment to honor those who have fallen in the battle against the demons. Their sacrifices will not be forgotten, and they serve as a reminder of the stakes of the battle they are about to face.

With their fleet ready and their resolve firm, Eli, James, Biggs, Josias, Adonis, and Ethan prepare to take to the skies and confront Babylon, hoping this will turn the tide in the war. They know that the battle ahead will be the most difficult they have ever faced, but they are prepared to give everything they must to protect humanity and rid the world of the demonic threat.

As they board their planes and prepare to take off, they think to the battle ahead, knowing they may not all make it out alive. But they are united in their mission and ready to face whatever challenges come their way. With a final salute to their fallen comrades, they take to the skies, ready to confront their destiny and bring an end to the Babylon's reign of terror, determined to defeat him and his minions.

As Josias and Biggs fine-tune the fighter mech, ensuring every component is in optimal condition for the battle ahead, they share a silent understanding of the gravity of the situation. They know that they must be at their best if they hope to stand a chance against Babylon and his forces. Meanwhile, Gage and Hunter stand vigil over their injured comrades, their determination unwavering despite the daunting task ahead. They are acutely aware of the formidable adversaries they face, including Lucifer himself, and the magnitude of the battle that lies before them.

As they prepare themselves mentally and physically for the coming confrontation, they draw strength from their bond as brothers and their shared determination to emerge victorious. With the fate of humanity on the line, they know they must give everything they have and more to defeat the forces of darkness and restore peace to the world.

Mike's awakening brings a sense of relief and renewed hope to the team. As they gather around him, they share moments of joy and laughter, grateful for his recovery and the chance to fight alongside him once again. Despite the daunting task ahead and the uncertainties they face, they draw strength from their camaraderie and determination to confront the forces of darkness head-on.

With Mike back in the fold, the team feels more prepared and unified than ever. They know they must face the challenges ahead together, relying on each other's strengths and unwavering resolve. As they continue to prepare for the impending battle, they are fueled by the belief that, no matter what obstacles they may encounter, they will face them with courage and determination.

As Mike begins to share his dream with Josias and the rest of the team, a sense of reverence and anticipation fills the air. They listen intently, hanging on to his every word, recognizing the significance of his vision and its potential implications for their mission.

In his dream, Mike recounts a powerful presence, a celestial being who transcends mortal understanding, guiding and protecting them on their journey. Despite the challenges they face and the dangers that lie ahead, this divine presence assures them they are not alone, instilling them in courage and faith.

As Mike speaks, his words resonate deeply with each member of the team, reinforcing their resolve and strengthening their belief in their cause. They understand that their mission is not just about defeating the forces of darkness, but also about upholding the values of courage, unity, and hope.

With renewed purpose and a sense of divine guidance, the team prepares to face whatever challenges may come their way, knowing they carry with them the support of someone greater than themselves. They stand united, ready to confront the darkness and restore light to the world once more.

As Mike shares the details of his dream, a hushed reverence falls over the group, each member hanging on to his every word. They listen intently, captivated by the profound message conveyed in his vision.

In the dream, Mike describes being summoned forth by a voice that emanated authority and reassurance, guiding him forward with a sense of purpose and urgency. He recalls encountering figures who felt familiar yet enigmatic, their presence imbued with significance beyond his comprehension.

The message delivered to him resonates deeply with the team, affirming their mission and calling them to action against the forces of darkness that threaten to engulf their world. They understand that they are not alone in their struggle but supported by a divine presence who empowers and protects them.

As Mike concludes his account, a sense of determination fills the air, each member of the team fortified by the knowledge that they are part of something greater than themselves. With renewed resolve, they prepare to face their destiny, ready to confront the challenges ahead with courage and conviction.

Mike's revelation leaves the group in awe, each member processing the weight of the message delivered to him in his dream. The idea of chosen individuals among them, destined to confront the great evil of Babylon and restore balance to their world, fills them with a mixture of determination and reverence.

Gage's silent prayer, heard by Mike within the depths of his vision, underscores the mysterious connection they share and the divine guidance guiding their path forward. The notion of divine intervention and the presence of a higher power instills them with a newfound sense of purpose and resolve.

As they reflect on the significance of Mike's experience, a sense of unity and purpose washes over the group, strengthening their resolve to face whatever challenges lie ahead. With faith in their hearts and a shared determination to fulfill their destiny, they stand ready to confront the darkness and emerge victorious in the battle to come.

"Why?" Charlie cannot help but ask, his outburst reflecting a common human sentiment as he questions the existence of higher powers and their apparent lack of intervention in times of crisis. His frustration stems from the suffering endured by humanity in the face of evil and chaos, despite his belief in a benevolent creator.

Biggs attempts to provide reassurance by suggesting there is a purpose behind every event, even if it is not immediately apparent. He implies that challenges and suffering may serve as opportunities for growth, learning, and redemption.

But despite Biggs' attempt to offer solace, Charlie's frustration persists as he grapples with the injustice and arbitrary nature of their plight. His question of "why?" echoes the existential inquiry of countless individuals throughout history who have struggled to reconcile their faith with the harsh realities of the world.

As the group contemplates Charlie's question, they are reminded of the complexity of the human experience and the enduring quest for meaning and understanding in the face of adversity. Their collective journey toward enlightenment and resolution will continue as they confront the challenges before them, seeking answers and redemption in a world fraught with darkness and uncertainty.

Emergence

They take turns resting and keeping watch, a smart strategy to ensure everyone stays alert and ready for the upcoming battle. It is crucial for them to conserve their energy and maintain their mental clarity amidst the ongoing darkness and uncertainty. By prioritizing rest and maintaining vigilance, they can maximize their chances of success when the time comes to confront their adversaries.

Charlie's reflections touch on a deep truth about humanity's struggles and the potential for redemption through unity and perseverance. It is a sobering realization that their own actions and resolutions could be the catalyst for divine intervention or assistance in their time of need. As they gear up for the battle ahead, Charlie's words serve as a reminder of the importance of resilience and solidarity in the face of adversity.

Mike's words reflect the surreal and intense nature of their situation, where they find themselves confronting mythical creatures and facing unimaginable challenges. The dream he had adds another layer of complexity to their reality, blurring the lines between the tangible and the supernatural.

As they prepare to face the unknown, Mike's uncertainty mirrors the uncertainty felt by all of them in the face of such daunting adversaries.

Mike's reflections delve into the existential questions surrounding their predicament. The idea of being chosen to fight against demonic forces evokes a sense of purpose and destiny, but it also raises doubts about the nature of those who may have orchestrated such events. The ambiguity of their situation leaves them grappling with the unknown, questioning whether there is a divine plan at play or if they are merely pawns in a larger scheme. The mysteries of their circumstances remain unresolved, adding to the complexity of their journey.

The camaraderie between Mike and Gage shines through as they share a moment of levity amidst the chaos and stress of their situation. Their brotherly bond provides them with a source of strength and reassurance as they prepare to face the challenges ahead. Despite the pain and hardships they have endured, their connection remains unbreakable, serving as a reminder of the importance of unity in the face of adversity. Gage confirms that everything is indeed ready to go and they can proceed with assessing the fighters and their functions. They have checked all available systems to ensure they are functioning correctly and are prepared for action. With their preparations complete, they are ready to put the fighters to the test and ensure they are fully operational for the upcoming battle against the forces of darkness.

Josias pushes the fighter to its maximum speed, everyone watching in great suspense, admiring the skill and daring of their friend and family members. Eli listens intently to the radio receiver, his heart pounding with a mixture of pride and worry for his son's safety. James, Gage, Mike, Hunter, Charlie, and the rest of the group hold their breath as they witness the fighter streaking across the sky, leaving behind a trail of awe and admiration.

As Josias reaches supersonic speeds, the fighter becomes a mere blur, disappearing instantaneously. Eli communicates with Josias via radio, urging him to be cautious and mindful of his limits. James, sensing the tension among the group, encourages them to marvel at the spectacle of Josias's flight, albeit with a hint of concern lingering in his voice.

With his fingers crossed, Josias accelerates the fighter to five times the speed of sound, propelling it into the realm of near invisibility. In a matter of seconds, the aircraft becomes a fleeting apparition, leaving everyone astounded by its incredible velocity and agility. As they mark the position and speed of the fighter, they can only hope and pray for Josias's safe return from his exhilarating test flight.

As Josias brings the fighter out of top speed and begins to descend, a resounding boom echoes through the air, signaling his return from the exhilarating test flight. James and Biggs exchange glances, their expressions reflecting a mix of relief and anticipation as they watch the fighter approach the runway.

Emergence

Eli rushes to the edge of the runway, his heart pounding with a mixture of anxiety and pride. As Josias expertly guides the fighter back to the surface, his father's face breaks into a wide grin of relief. With precision and finesse, Josias brings the aircraft to a gentle landing, the roar of its engines gradually subsiding.

Eli rushes forward to greet his son, his eyes shining with pride and joy. As Josias steps out of the cockpit, he is saluted with cheers and applause from his family and friends, their worries evaporating in the wake of his safe return.

James, Biggs, and the rest of the group gather around Josias, congratulating him on his successful test flight. Amidst the excitement and relief, they exchange smiles and words of encouragement, grateful for Josias's skill and courage in the face of danger.

With Josias back on solid ground, the group cannot help but feel a renewed sense of determination and readiness for the battles that lie ahead. As they prepare for the challenges to come, they know that with Josias at the helm, they stand a fighting chance against whatever darkness may threaten their world.

As Josias recounts his harrowing journey to New York City, the group listens intently, their expressions shifting from excitement to concern. Adonis's exhilaration quickly gives way to a somber realization of the enormity of the task ahead. Biggs furrows his brow, processing Josias's words. "So, you're saying Babylon has a massive army at his disposal? That's not going to be an easy fight."

Josias nods grimly. "Exactly. We are talking about a formidable force, and they are not going to go down quietly. But we cannot let that discourage us. We have the strength and the determination to take them on, no matter how daunting the odds may seem."

Eli steps forward, his eyes reflecting the weight of the situation. "We've faced challenges before, and we've always come out on top. This will be no different. We'll strategize, we'll fight smart, and we'll stand together as a family."

Emergence

The group nods in agreement, their resolve hardened by the gravity of the task before them. Despite the overwhelming odds, they know that with unity and determination, they can overcome any obstacle in their path.

As they prepare to face the looming threat of Babylon and his army, they draw strength from each other, ready to confront whatever dangers may come their way. With Josias leading the charge, they stand ready to fight for the future of humanity.

Josias's warning sends a chill through the group, prompting them to spring into action. They quickly mobilize, arming themselves to the teeth and fortifying their defenses against any potential threat.

Eli takes charge, coordinating the efforts to secure their weapons and fortify their position. "We can't afford to take any chances," he declares, his voice firm with determination. "If Babylon's forces come knocking, we'll be ready for them."

The group works with precision and efficiency, ensuring that every weapon is operational and loaded, and every mech and fighter prepared for battle. They stand united, ready to defend their home and their loved ones against any enemy that dares to threaten them.

As they await the inevitable confrontation with Babylon's forces, their resolve remains unshakable. With their weapons ready and their spirits fortified, they stand as a formidable force against the encroaching darkness.

Josias nods in understanding as his father Eli reassures him, the weight of responsibility heavy on his shoulders. With determination in their hearts, they set aside their worries and focus on the task at hand: preparing for the impending battle. Together, they work tirelessly to ensure that every weapon is fully charged and every fighter is ready for action. There is a sense of urgency in the air as they position their defenses, knowing that the fate of their loved ones and their world hangs in the balance.

Emergence

As they labor through the night, their resolve only grows stronger. They may be facing an impossible enemy, but they refuse to back down. With their weapons armed and their fighters ready, they stand united against the darkness, ready to fight for their freedom and their future.

As the team quickly moves to execute Eli's plan, tension hangs heavy in the air as they face the daunting task ahead. Each member understands the urgency of their mission and works swiftly to place the blue tag C4 in strategic locations throughout the airport.

Josias and Biggs head to the west wing, carefully placing the C4 on the gas pipes, while Ethan and Adonis descend into the basement to target critical utility lines. Hunter and Gage move to the north, preparing to ignite the C4 upon the first fighter's takeoff, while Mike, Charlie, Eli, and James cover the south and east sides of the airport, ensuring every inch is outfitted to explode.

However, their efforts are interrupted by the ominous sight of a swarm of demonized creatures descending upon them from the sky. The team braces themselves for the impending battle, knowing their mission to destroy the airport and eliminate the demon knights has just become even more urgent and dangerous. With determination in their hearts and explosives in hand, they prepare to face the enemy, ready to fight for their survival and the safety of their loved ones.

Josias quickly thinks on his feet, realizing they need a plan to take down the demon knights without the C4 they were counting on. He glances around, searching for any available resources they can use to their advantage. Spotting a nearby fuel tank, Josias formulates a risky plan.

"Biggs, follow me," Josias whispers urgently. "We're going to lure them towards that fuel tank. We'll use it to create a distraction and take out as many of them as we can."

With a nod of understanding, Biggs follows Josias's lead as they stealthily make their way toward the fuel tank. They position themselves strategically, waiting for the demon knights to approach. As the enemy draws near, Josias and

Emergence

Biggs spring into action, igniting the fuel tank with a well-placed shot.

The explosion rips through the air, engulfing the demon knights in a fiery blast. Josias and Biggs take advantage of the chaos, swiftly eliminating any remaining threats with precise shots from their weapons.

Breathing heavily but triumphant, Josias and Biggs regroup, ready to continue their fight against the demons. With quick thinking and teamwork, they have managed to turn the tide of the battle in their favor, proving that, even in the face of overwhelming odds, they refuse to back down.

As Josias and Biggs lunge into action, they unleash a torrent of firepower upon the demon knights, determined to protect their loved ones and defeat the demonic invaders. With precise shots and strategic movements, they manage to neutralize the immediate threat, sending the demons reeling from the onslaught of bullets and explosions.

Biggs rushes to assist their father, Eli, while Josias heads toward Ethan and Adonis, who are engaged in their own struggle against the demon knights. Meanwhile, Mike and Gage stand their ground, fending off the relentless attacks of the enemy.

Together, they form a united front against the demonic forces, refusing to let fear or despair overcome them. With courage and determination, they fight back, each member of the team supporting and protecting one another in the heat of battle.

As the battle rages on, they remain steadfast in their resolve, knowing that their strength lies not just in their individual skills, but in their unwavering bond as a family.

And as they continue to fight side by side, they stand as a beacon of hope amidst the darkness, ready to face whatever challenges lie ahead.

Despite their injuries and the relentless assault from the demon knights, Mike and Gage stand their ground, refusing to surrender their souls or give in to fear. With fierce determination and a relentless spirit, they fight back against the demonic horde, unleashing a barrage of bullets and sheer force to push back their attackers.

As they battle through the chaos, each blow and wound only fuels their resolve to protect their loved ones and emerge victorious. Despite the odds stacked against them, they stand as a testament to the strength and resilience of the human spirit in the face of darkness and despair.

Their unwavering courage and determination inspire those around them to keep fighting, even as the battle rages on. With every step forward, they push through the pain and continue to fight, knowing their survival depends on it.

As they join their cousins in the fray, they lock eyes with each other, sharing a silent understanding and determination to overcome whatever challenges lie ahead. With their weapons at the ready and their spirits unbroken, they press forward, ready to face whatever comes their way with unwavering resolve and determination.

As the chaos unfolds around them, the family fights with an almost primal ferocity, determined to protect each other and their world from the demonic invaders. Covered in blood and surrounded by the fallen, they stand as a testament to the strength and resilience of the human spirit.

As they prepare to take to the skies and face the Great Dragon Babylon, they share a moment of camaraderie and determination, ready to confront the forces of hell head-on. But as they prepare to depart they encounter a lone demon knight, offering cryptic words about the true nature of their world and the presence of demons among them.

Unfazed by the demon knight's threats, they stand firm in their resolve, refusing to surrender their souls or succumb to fear.

As Josias streaks toward New York City at breakneck speed, his father Eli listens intently to his voice over the radio, relieved to hear his son's assurance that he is on his way.

With determination in their hearts, Eli and the others prepare to follow Josias into battle against the dragon Babylon.

Emergence

***

Meanwhile, in New York City, the explosion at Stewart Airport sends shockwaves through the air, catching the attention of all who witness it, including Babylon and his demonic minions. They understand the message loud and clear: a war is coming, and they will face fierce opposition from those who dare to challenge their tyranny.

As the stage is set for an epic showdown between humanity and the forces of hell, Eli and his family, along with their allies, brace themselves for the ultimate confrontation. The fate of the world hangs in the balance as they prepare to confront the ancient evil that threatens to consume everything in its path.

As the demon knights fly toward the sky, anticipating victory after the destruction at Stewart Airport, a sudden and unexpected sight fills the air. People on the ground watch in awe as a swarm of evil angels is quickly intercepted by a group flying toward them at incredible speed.

Amidst the chaos, a plane emerges from hypersonic speed, catching the attention of those on the ground who had lost hope after the airport explosion. It becomes evident that despite the devastation, remnants of the military remain, determined to stand against the forces of hell and protect humanity from the impending threat.

As the mech fighter unleashes its devastating payload, the miniature missiles find their targets with deadly accuracy, causing explosions that rip through the ranks of the demon knights. The people on the ground, witnessing this display of firepower, find renewed hope in the face of the demonic onslaught.

However, the demon knights quickly retaliate, using their formidable abilities to counter the attack. With powerful beams of energy emitted from their eyes and fiery projectiles launched from their hands, they aim to destroy the Mech Fighters and anyone else who stands in their way.

Emergence

Despite the fierce resistance, the fighters heroically press forward, determined to defend humanity against the forces of hell.

As Babylon roars with fury, the skies respond with thunder and lightning and a torrent of blood-like rain begins to fall, obscuring the view for those below. People scramble for cover, while others watch in awe as the demon knights face off against the stealth fighters in the crimson downpour. Unbeknownst to Babylon, the fighters activate their stealth mode, rendering them invisible to the naked eye.

Despite the blinding rain, the fighters rely on advanced technology to target their enemies, using heat signatures and other sensors to track the demon knights with precision.

In the darkness of the storm, the fighters unleash their firepower, swiftly eliminating the demons with deadly efficiency. Babylon seethe with anger as he watches his warriors fall from the sky, realizing that their failure may anger his master, Lucifer.

Meanwhile, on the ground, people salvage whatever they can from the fallen demon knights, preparing for whatever may come next in this battle for survival against the forces of hell.

As Josias maneuvers his stealth fighter in an attempt to shake off the demon knights clinging to his wings, he hears the tearing of metal and feels the imbalance caused by their presence. Determined to rid his aircraft of the unwelcome passengers, he executes evasive maneuvers, performing barrel rolls in an effort to dislodge them.

One of the demon knights loses its grip and falls away from the fighter, but the other remains stubbornly attached to the wing, continuing to tear at the metal. Despite Josias's efforts to outmaneuver it, the demon persists in its destructive actions, posing a threat to the integrity of the aircraft.

In the midst of this struggle, another aircraft, piloted by Biggs, approaches Josias's fighter head-on, engaging in a dangerous game of chicken. With the demon still clinging to Josias' wing and the incoming threat from Babylon, Josias faces a critical moment in the ongoing battle against the forces of hell.

Adonis also finds himself in a desperate aerial battle, and he pushes the limits of his piloting skills, maneuvering the fighter in ways he never imagined possible. Weaving through the demon knights' attacks, he dodges their hellish powers, moving swiftly from side to side to avoid their onslaught. He engages the enemy with precision, unleashing his mini missiles to devastating effect, taking out multiple demons with each pass. But as he maneuvers closer to his targets, one of the demon knights manages to graze the underside of his wing, sending his aircraft into a dangerous spiral.

With the plane spinning out of control, Ethan advises Adonis over the radio to engage the after thrusters to stabilize the descent. Despite his frantic attempts to activate the thrusters, Adonis finds himself unable to regain control, facing imminent disaster as two powerful demon knights close in on him.

Faced with the prospect of certain death, Adonis's desperation turns to rage as he grabs hold of the fighter's weapons, prepared to make a final stand. But just as he prepares to engage the enemy the after thrusters suddenly roar to life, propelling him upward and away from the imminent threat.

However, as he escapes the deadly grasp of the demon knights, one of them unleashes a powerful blast of energy, melting a hole in the cockpit glass and nearly sending Adonis hurtling out of the sky. Despite the harrowing ordeal, Adonis manages to regain control of the fighter, narrowly avoiding disaster as he continues to battle against the forces of hell in the bloody skies.

As Ethan and James continue their aerial maneuvers, they find themselves in a perilous situation when Babylon unleashes a burst of fire from his mouth, aimed directly at their planes. With quick thinking and precise coordination, Ethan instructs James to lean left, narrowly avoiding the fiery attack.

Emergence

Their planes graze at the edge of the fireball, the intense heat melting the metal underneath but not enough to bring them crashing down. As they emerge unscathed from the narrow escape, James expresses his gratitude to Ethan for his quick reflexes, acknowledging that it was indeed a narrow escape. Ethan reassures James, emphasizing that as long as they both stay alive, the debt has already been repaid. The camaraderie between the two pilots strengthens their resolve as they continue to face the onslaught of demon knights in the skies above, their determination unwavering in the face of danger. Eli finds himself in a dangerous situation as he is followed by demon knights armed with deadly projectiles and powers, but with quick thinking and skillful maneuvering he employs a daring tactic to turn the tables on his pursuers. Using his fighter's afterburner, Eli scorches one of the demon knights attempting to grab onto his plane, then swiftly evades the others with agile maneuvers.

Employing his arsenal of heat-seeking missiles, Eli takes out multiple demons in midair, their fiery demise leaving a trail of destruction in their wake. However, one particularly resilient demon knight manages to survive, launching a desperate counterattack against Eli's fighter.

Throwing spiked bones and activating his onboard mini missile gun, the demon knight unleashes a barrage of attacks aimed at Eli's plane. Despite the intense assault, Eli remains determined, navigating his fighter through the onslaught while devising a strategy to eliminate his relentless adversary.

Hunter and Charlie's synchronized aerial maneuvers impress onlookers below, who marvel at their skill and coordination amidst the chaos of battle. The brothers' seamless teamwork allows them to fend off demon knights from multiple directions, turning the fight into a high-stakes game of cat and mouse in the skies above. As they switch positions to cover each other's backs, their camaraderie and determination shine through, inspiring hope in those witnessing their bravery from the ground.

Emergence

As Babylon redirects his attention toward Josias and Eli, the people on the ground scramble for cover, fearing the wrath of the demonic dragon. However, they find solace and renewed hope in the sight of Josias and Eli's relentless assault on Babylon. The ground shakes as the fighters unleash their firepower, creating a barrage of explosions that rock the area. Babylon roars in fury as he attempts to defend himself against the onslaught, his massive form trembling under the impact of the attacks.

The people watch with apprehensive hope, praying for the fighters' success as they continue to battle against the forces of darkness in a desperate bid to protect humanity.

As Josias and Eli evade Babylon's attack by luring him to chomp down on his own minions, Biggs watches in awe at their bravery and quick thinking. He expresses admiration for their actions, likening them to heroic madmen deserving recognition for their selfless acts. However, Eli humbly reminds Biggs that what they truly deserve is peace, freedom, and hope for a better future, not merely material accolades that may fade with time. It is a poignant moment of reflection amidst the chaos of battle, emphasizing the importance of their struggle for the greater good.

As everyone realizes their fuel is running low and Babylon's frustration grows, the battle intensifies. Babylon starts hurling fiery spears at the mech fighters, nearly hitting Gage, who manages to restart his engines just in time. With renewed determination, Gage rejoins the fight alongside his brother, Mike. Despite their exhaustion, the fighters press on, facing endless waves of demon knights. Josias asks his father Eli about a plan if they run out of fuel, and Eli reveals a secret military airport in North Carolina known only to top officials. As they prepare to make their escape, Josias urges everyone to unleash a barrage of homing missiles at Babylon, signaling that they will not be conquered so easily. With their message sent, the fighters accelerate to hypersonic speed, leaving Babylon behind in their wake.

Emergence

Amidst the chaos and destruction, the resilience of humanity shines through. Despite the overwhelming presence of demon knights and the stench of death permeating the air, people on the ground remain steadfast in their reality, refusing to succumb to the terror unleashed by these creatures. They recognize the twisted transformation of once-beautiful beings into grotesque entities, a stark reminder of the evil that now plagues the earth. Yet, amidst the darkness, there is still beauty to be found in the world and in humanity itself. The earth is not just a gift but a birthright, entrusted to humankind to cherish and protect.

Though faced with unimaginable challenges, humans stand united in their determination to defend their home and preserve its splendor. Just as the celestial beings watch over them from above, it is their duty to safeguard the beauty of the world they inhabit. In the face of adversity, humanity's resilience and strength shine brightly, a testament to their enduring spirit.

Despite the looming threat of torture and torment, the people who have escaped the bloody rain find a newfound sense of unity and determination. They refuse to cower in fear before the evil forces that seek to dominate their world.

Instead, they rally together, knowing their collective strength and resilience will be their greatest weapon against the darkness that surrounds them.

As they plot and strategize in the shadows, they draw inspiration from the brave souls who continue to fight against the demons and their monstrous master. The sight of fellow humans standing up to the forces of evil fills them with hope and courage, spurring them on to resist and defy their oppressors at any cost.

Even as Babylon threatens them with unimaginable horrors, they remain steadfast in their resolve, refusing to surrender their freedom and their spirits to the darkness. They know

Emergence

that they must stand together and fight for the sake of their souls, their loved ones, and the future of their world.

Though the odds may seem insurmountable, the indomitable spirit of humanity burns bright, ready to face whatever challenges may come their way. As they prepare to confront the entrenched evil, they cling to the hope that their courage and determination will prevail against the forces of darkness.

The gruesome scene unfolds as the hellhounds from Babylon's throne descend upon the terrified people, unleashing their savage fury upon them. Each victim's screams of agony echo through the air, a chilling reminder of the horrors that await those who dare to defy the great dragon and his minions.

The first hellhound shows no mercy as it savagely tears into a helpless woman, its fiery saliva melting her flesh and bones as if they were nothing more than paper. With each bite the woman's cries of pain grow louder, her futile attempts to defend herself only met with further torment and suffering. In the end, her body is nothing but a lifeless husk, consumed by the merciless jaws of the hellhound.

Meanwhile, the second hellhound toys with its prey, relishing in the chase before finally descending upon a helpless man with brutal efficiency. Its powerful jaws rip through flesh and bone, leaving behind a trail of devastation as the man's life is cruelly snuffed out by the fiery hound.

As the hellhounds feast upon their victims, the people cower in fear, knowing they are powerless against the relentless onslaught of the forces of darkness. With each passing moment, hope seems to fade further away, replaced only by despair and dread.

But amidst the chaos and carnage, there are those who refuse to surrender to despair, those who still cling to the flickering flame of hope in their hearts. Though the odds may seem insurmountable, they know they must stand strong and fight against the darkness, for it is only through unity and determination that they can hope to overcome the evil that threatens to consume them all.

Emergence

***

Babylon's laughter echoes through the darkened skies as he observes the carnage wrought by his hellhounds upon the hapless victims below. In his twisted mind, he relishes in the suffering of the mortals, taking perverse pleasure in their torment.

However, his amusement quickly turns to frustration as he realizes he may have underestimated the threat posed by the flying machines. In his arrogance he had sent the hellhounds to deal with the humans on the ground, believing them to be the greater threat. Now, as he watches the relentless onslaught of the mech fighters in the sky, he begins to understand the folly of his decision.

With a growl of frustration, Babylon curses his own arrogance, realizing he may have made a grave mistake. The flying machines, with their advanced weaponry and formidable pilots, pose a far greater threat than he had anticipated. If he does not act quickly, they could spell doom for him and his plans to conquer the world.

Determined to rectify his error, Babylon summons his remaining forces and prepares to engage the flying machines in battle. Though the odds may seem stacked against him, he knows he cannot afford to falter now.

The fate of the world hangs in the balance, and he will stop at nothing to emerge victorious.

***

Three people huddle together, trembling in fear as they face the monstrous hellhound, its fiery gaze piercing through their souls. A fat man, a skinny woman, and a child cling to each other, their hearts pounding with terror as they await their gruesome fate.

Suddenly, the fat man steps forward, his voice shaking but defiant. He tells the hellhound that if it wants a meal, it will have to go through him first. The skinny woman and the child look at him in astonishment, unsure whether to admire his bravery or despair at his foolishness.

The hellhound snarls, its jaws dripping with saliva as it inches closer to the defiant man. But before it can strike, a voice echoes through the darkness, commanding the hellhound to stop.

Everyone turns to see a figure emerging from the shadows, clad in armor and wielding a gleaming sword. It is a warrior, determined to protect the innocent from the clutches of evil. With a swift motion the warrior charges at the hellhound, engaging it in a fierce battle. The fat man, the skinny woman, and the child watch in awe as the warrior fights with unmatched skill and bravery, driving the hellhound back with each strike of his sword.

In the end, it is the warrior who emerges victorious, vanquishing the hellhound and saving the lives of the three people. They thank him profusely, grateful for his courage and heroism in their darkest hour.

As the warrior stands victorious amidst the wreckage, his heart filled with a sense of purpose and duty, he knows his battle against the forces of evil is far from over. But with each victory he brings hope to those who have lost everything, reminding them that even in the face of darkness, there is always light.

Another scene is one of utter horror and despair as a hellhound mercilessly claims its victims, leaving behind only destruction and death in its wake. A man's desperate attempt to flee with a child ends in tragedy as they are both overtaken by the relentless pursuit of the hellhound.

The child's agonizing screams fill the air as the hellhound sinks its razor-sharp claws into his flesh, tearing away chunks of his young body. The man, paralyzed with fear, can only watch in horror as his companion is brutally massacred, knowing there is little he can do to save him.

As the hellhound turns its attention to the man, there is a moment of hopelessness as he realizes the futility of his efforts to escape. In a cruel twist of fate, he too becomes prey to the insatiable hunger of the hellhound, his life extinguished in a matter of moments.

The carnage left behind by the hellhound serves as a chilling reminder of the relentless power of evil, leaving those who witness it shaken to their core. In the face of such darkness, the survivors can only cling to each other, praying for deliverance from the surrounding horrors.

The scene is one of unspeakable horror and devastation as the hellhounds continue their merciless rampage, leaving a trail of destruction and despair in their wake. The sheer brutality of their attacks is evident as they tear into their victims with savage ferocity, leaving behind only death and suffering.

The once-hopeful atmosphere has been shattered by the relentless onslaught of the hellhounds, the survivors left reeling in shock and terror. The smell of burning sulfur fills the air, mingling with the agonized screams of the dying and creating an atmosphere of pure dread and despair.

For those who witness the carnage, there is no escape from the overwhelming sense of hopelessness. Death is the only way out, as the hellhounds show no mercy to their victims, leaving behind nothing but devastation and destruction in their wake.

In the face of such unimaginable horror, the survivors can only cling to each other, seeking solace and comfort in their shared suffering. But as the hellhounds continue their relentless onslaught, the future looks bleak and uncertain, death looming over them like a dark shadow.

One man's act of bravery amidst the chaos is both commendable and foolhardy. As he charges out to confront the hellhound, fueled by righteous anger and a desire to protect those who cannot protect themselves, he embodies the spirit of defiance against the forces of darkness.

However, facing off against such a formidable adversary with nothing but a steel pipe is a daunting task, and the man's chances of success are uncertain. While his initial strike momentarily incapacitates the hellhound, it is unlikely to be enough to permanently defeat the creature.

Nevertheless, the man's courage serves as a beacon of hope for those witnessing the carnage unfold. In a world overrun by terror and despair, his willingness to stand up and fight against the forces of evil inspires others to resist, even in the face of overwhelming odds.

As the man prepares to face the hellhound head-on, he knows that the outcome is bleak. But in this moment of desperation he refuses to back down, determined to do whatever it takes to protect those he cares about and strike a blow against the darkness that threatens to consume them all.

The man's attempt to strike the hellhound once again with the steel pipe proves futile as the intense heat emanating from the creature's burning body causes the metal to disintegrate into ash. In his desperation to defend himself and those around him, he is met with the harsh reality of the hellhound's infernal nature, a force beyond the limits of mortal weapons.

As the steel pipe turns to nothing in his hands, the man realizes the dire situation he faces. With his makeshift weapon rendered useless, he stands before the hellhound, defenseless against its fury. Yet, despite the overwhelming odds stacked against him, he refuses to cower in fear or surrender to despair.

In this moment of crisis, the unknown man's resolve is tested to its limits. With the hellhound bearing down on him, he knows his only chance of survival lies in his courage and resourcefulness. He must find a way to outwit or outmaneuver the beast, relying on his instincts and determination to outlast the onslaught of darkness.

As the man braces himself for the impending confrontation, his heart pounds with adrenaline, his mind racing to find a strategy to overcome the insurmountable challenge before him. With every fiber of his being, he prepares to face the hellhound, refusing to yield to the terror threatening to consume him.

Emergence

As the man finds himself surrounded by hellhounds his heart sinks with despair, realizing the direness of his situation. With nowhere to run and no hope of escape, he feels the weight of fear pressing down upon him, threatening to smother him entirely. In his desperation, he continues to plead for divine intervention, calling out to his god with fervent prayers for deliverance from the horrors that encircle him.

With each passing moment the hellhounds draw closer, their eyes gleaming with malevolent intent, their fiery breath casting an ominous glow upon the scene. The man knows his fate hangs in the balance, his life teetering on the edge of oblivion as he stands on the precipice of doom.

Yet, even in the face of imminent peril, he refuses to surrender to despair. Clinging to the last shreds of hope within him, he musters the strength to face his fate with courage and resilience. With a steely resolve, he braces himself for whatever may come, ready to confront the darkness with unwavering determination.

In this moment of desperation, the unknown man's faith becomes his shield, his prayers a beacon of light amid darkness. Though the odds may seem insurmountable, he refuses to yield to despair, trusting in the power of divine intervention to guide him through the darkest of times.

As the man's screams echo through the desolate landscape, his body wracked with unimaginable pain, those who witness the gruesome spectacle recoil in horror, their stomachs churning at the sight before them. The hellhounds revel in their cruel victory, their laughter ringing out like a sinister symphony of torment.

Unable to bear the grisly scene unfolding before them, dozens of onlookers turn away, retching uncontrollably as they struggle to process the sheer brutality of the hellhounds' attack. The stench of death hangs heavy in the air, mingling with the acrid scent of burning flesh and the metallic tang of blood.

Emergence

Despite the overwhelming despair that grips the hearts of those who bear witness to the man's suffering, there is nothing they can do to intervene. Trapped in a nightmare of their own making, they are powerless to stop the relentless onslaught of the hellhounds.

As the man's lifeblood stains the ground beneath him, his anguished cries fading into the darkness, a sense of profound sorrow settles over those who remain. In the face of such unspeakable horror, they can only pray for deliverance from the relentless forces of darkness ready to consume them.

As the hellhounds advance, their fiery eyes scanning the surroundings for their next victim, panic grips the hearts of those who cower in hiding. The crackling of flames and the ominous growls of the hellhounds fill the air, heightening the sense of terror that hangs over the scene like a dark cloud. With each step the hellhounds take, the tension mounts, their predatory instincts guiding them unerringly toward their quarry. The people trapped within the confines of their hiding places can only pray for salvation, their breath caught in their throats as they await the inevitable confrontation.

Suddenly, one of the hellhounds catches sight of movement within a narrow crevice, its keen senses detecting the faintest hint of fear emanating from its prey. With a low growl it thrusts its snout into the opening, its hot breath sending shivers down the spine of the person trapped within.

As the seconds tick by, the tension reaches a fever pitch, each heartbeat echoing like a drumbeat of impending doom. The people hold their breath, praying for a miracle to spare them from the clutches of the hellhounds and the fiery fate that awaits them.

But in the end, there is no escape from the relentless march of darkness that now descends upon them. With a final, chilling howl, the hellhounds close in on their prey, sealing their fate in the fiery jaws of hell.

A teenager inches closer to the hellhounds, their attention remains fixed on their grisly feast, their jaws tearing into the flesh of their victim with savage intensity. But the teenager's

Emergence

bravado falters as he realizes the futility of his actions, the enormity of the danger he now faces dawning upon him. Despite his fear, the teenager's desperation drives him forward, fueled by a reckless defiance that borders on madness. He hurls insults and projectiles at the hellhounds, his voice trembling with a mixture of rage and fear.

But the hellhounds pay him no heed, their focus consumed by the carnage before them. They seem unaffected by the teenager's attempts to provoke them, their attention rigidly fixed on their meal.

As the teenager draws nearer, the air crackles with tension, the grim inevitability of his fate hanging heavy in the air. With each step he inches closer to the gaping maws of the hellhounds, their fiery eyes glinting with hunger and malice. In a final, desperate bid for survival, the teenager lunges forward, hoping to evade the hellhounds' notice and escape their clutches. But his efforts are in vain, his fate sealed by the merciless jaws of the hellhounds as they turn their attention to their next victim, leaving nothing but silence and despair in their wake.

The gruesome scene unfolds before the horrified onlookers, their faces contorted in a mixture of disgust, shock, and fear. The teenager's reckless actions have cost him dearly, his body now laid bare before the relentless hellhounds, a grim testament to the unforgiving nature of their wrath.

As the teenager collapses to the ground, his entrails spilling out in a pool of blood and gore, a hushed silence falls over the crowd. Those in the general area recoil in horror, unable to bear the sight of such brutality, while others avert their gaze, unwilling to acknowledge the gruesome sight before them.

Whispers of disbelief and condemnation ripple through the crowd as they grapple with the harrowing spectacle unfolding before their eyes. The teenager's foolish bravado has led to his untimely demise, a grim reminder of the deadly consequences of challenging the ferocious hellhounds.

Emergence

As the hellhounds continue their macabre feast, the people watch on in stunned silence, a sense of dread settling over them like a shroud. The teenager's fate serves as a chilling warning, a stark reminder of the perilous world they now inhabit, where even the slightest provocation can result in swift and merciless retribution.

The remaining survivors, paralyzed with fear, know they have no choice but to comply with the dragon's chilling ultimatum. As they emerge from their hiding places, their faces pale with terror, they cast fearful glances at the towering figure of Babylon, his eyes blazing with malevolent fury.

With trembling hands and quivering voices, they plead for mercy, their desperate cries echoing through the desolate landscape. But Babylon remains unmoved, his heart as cold as the depths of hell itself.

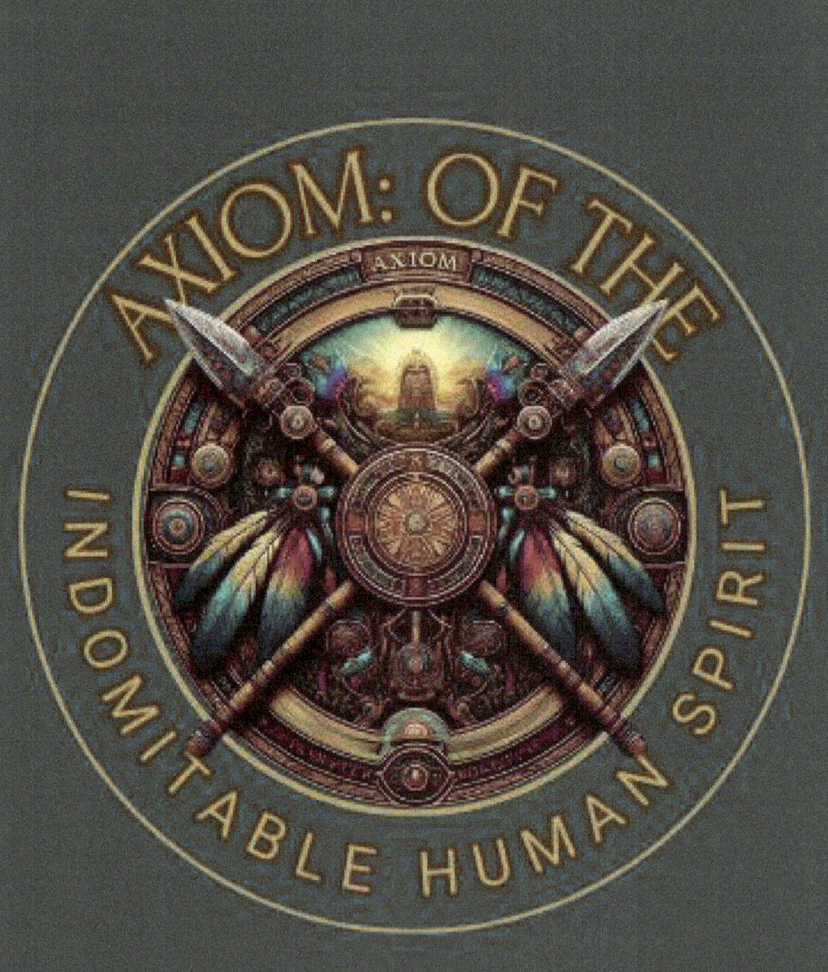

AXIOM: OF THE
INDOMITABLE HUMAN SPIRIT
AXIOM

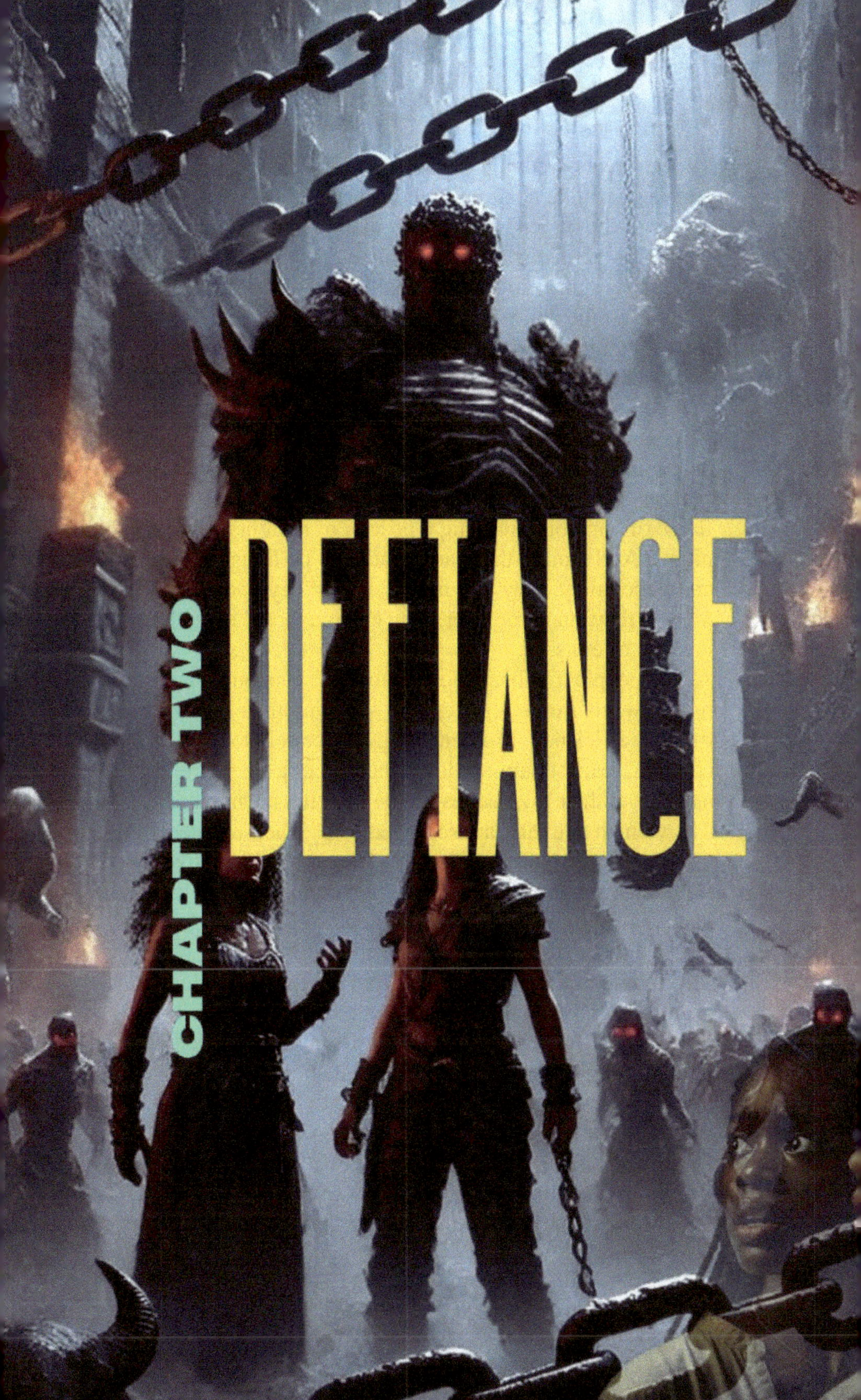

CHAPTER TWO
DEFIANCE

Defiance

The survivors are whipped together by Babylon's hellish angels, their fate hanging in the balance, their lives at the mercy of the merciless creatures that now surround them. Each moment feels like an eternity as they wait for the inevitable, their hearts heavy with dread and despair.

But amidst the darkness and despair, a flicker of defiance ignites within their souls. Though outnumbered and outmatched, they refuse to surrender to the forces of evil that seek to crush their spirits and extinguish their hope.

With newfound resolve, they stand together, united in their determination to resist the tyranny of Babylon and his minions. For even in the face of unimaginable horror, the flame of hope burns bright, a beacon of light in the darkest of nights. And though the road ahead may be fraught with peril and uncertainty, they will not falter, for they know that as long as they stand together, they can overcome even the greatest of evils.

As the people tremble in fear, Babylon's demonic angels move swiftly through the crowd, selecting their victims with ruthless efficiency. Mothers cling desperately to their children, tears streaming down their faces as they are torn apart from their loved ones by the merciless demons.

The women and girls are scourged away, their cries echoing through the desolate landscape as they are held captive by Babylon's minions. Their fate is uncertain, but they know that whatever awaits them in the depths of hell will be far worse than anything they have ever imagined.

Meanwhile, the remaining survivors are left to ponder their grim fate, knowing they are now at the mercy of the evilest forces in existence. With heavy hearts and souls filled with despair, they bow their heads in resignation, knowing there is little hope left for them in this world.

But amidst the darkness, a glimmer of defiance still burns within their hearts. Though they may be battered and broken, they refuse to surrender to the forces of evil. For as long as there is breath in their bodies, they will continue to fight for their freedom and the survival of their humanity, no matter the cost.

***

As the female captives enter the opulent throne room, they are overwhelmed by the sheer grandeur of their surroundings. The sparkling diamonds, gleaming crystals, and precious metals mock their plight, serving as a stark reminder of the contrast between their current situation and the beauty they once knew.

The sight of clear water offers a glimmer of hope amidst the darkness, drawing the weary captives toward its inviting surface. For a moment, they allow themselves to forget the horrors that surround them, basking in the simple pleasure of something as basic as water.

But their brief respite is shattered as the demon knights remind them of their true purpose—to serve the most ruthless and powerful of evil generals and their master. Despite their fear and desperation, the captives know that they have no choice but to comply with the wishes of their captors, lest they face even greater suffering.

As they prepare for the feast that awaits them, the captives exchange nervous glances, silently praying for a miracle to deliver them from this nightmare. But deep down they know that their fate lies in the hands of their merciless masters, and that escape may be nothing more than a distant dream.

Twenty women eagerly strip off their clothes and rush toward the glistening water, their excitement masking the underlying danger of their situation. They see the opportunity to bathe and enjoy a respite from their suffering as a welcome reprieve without fully comprehending the potential consequences of their actions.

Unaware of the sinister intentions that may lurk beneath the surface, they immerse themselves in the water, relishing in the sensation of cleansing and renewal. But little do they know that by indulging in this apparent luxury, they may be

Defiance

sealing their fates and binding themselves to a dark and malevolent force.

Their naive enthusiasm blinds them to the truth of their situation, and they eagerly embrace what they perceive as a momentary escape from their torment. However, the price they may pay for their moment of bliss could be far greater than they ever imagined. As they luxuriate in the soothing waters, oblivious to the unseen forces at play, their fate hangs in the balance, teetering on the edge of a precipice from which there may be no return.

Three other women stand before the demon knights, their defiance evident in their silence. Despite the allure of the water and the promise of respite, they remain steadfast in their refusal to partake in what they perceive as a blasphemous act.

Their refusal to engage in the bathing ritual reflects their staunch opposition to submitting to the will of their captors, even in the face of temptation and coercion. They would rather endure the consequences of their defiance than compromise their principles and dignity by succumbing to the demands of those who seek to subjugate them.

As they stand before the demons, their resolve is unyielding. They silently defy the oppressive forces seeking to impose their will upon them. Their refusal to comply serves as a testament to their inner strength and resilience, a defiance born from the depths of their spirits and forged in the crucible of adversity.

Though their future remains uncertain and the consequences of their defiance may be severe, they stand firm in their convictions, unwilling to betray their principles or surrender their autonomy to those who would seek to exploit and oppress them.

One of the demons studies them; it does not move, simply watching them. The three women, astonished by the demon's unexpected restraint, exchange puzzled glances, uncertain of the implications of its actions. Despite their initial fear, they

Defiance

find themselves intrigued by the demon's reluctance to harm them without explicit orders from a higher authority.

Their curiosity piqued, they cautiously observe the demon, searching for any clues that might shed light on its behavior. They speculate that there are limits to its power or constraints imposed upon him by its superiors. Alternatively, they consider the possibility that the demon may harbor its own reservations or conflicts of conscience which prevent it from conducting acts of violence without justification.

As they ponder these questions, the three women remain vigilant, wary of the demon's intentions yet intrigued by the enigma it presents. They resolve to remain vigilant and observant, determined to uncover the truth behind the unexpected behavior and discern any opportunities that may arise from this unforeseen turn of events.

***

A defiant woman's words echo through the chamber, resonating with a sense of defiance and hope amidst the despair of hell's dominion. Her proclamation serves as a rallying cry for those who refuse to succumb to the darkness, urging them to hold fast to their principles and resist the temptations of evil.

As the other women listen to her impassioned speech, they find courage in her words, bolstering their resolve to remain steadfast against the forces of darkness. Despite the overwhelming power of the demon knights and the allure of submission, they are inspired to cling to their humanity and hold to the belief that redemption and salvation are still within reach.

Though surrounded by the horrors of hell and faced with unimaginable suffering, these women refuse to abandon hope. Their collective defiance serves as a beacon of light amidst the shadows, a reminder that even in the darkest of times, the human spirit is capable of enduring and triumphing over adversity.

Defiance

As they stand united against the forces of evil, the women vow to continue their resistance, determined to defy the will of the Devil and his minions until the day they are either rescued, or their souls are released from the clutches of hell's grasp.

***

A woman meets the demon knight's gaze with unwavering determination, refusing to be intimidated by its words. She stands her ground, her eyes burning with opposition as she responds, telling the demon knight that her faith cannot be shaken by his lies and deception. She declares that even in the darkest of times, she will continue to believe in the power of goodness and righteousness, knowing that her God is always present, even in the depths of hell.

As the demon scoffs at her faith, the woman remains resolute, refusing to waver in her conviction. She knows that her beliefs are her strength, and she will not allow herself to be swayed by the words of a servant of darkness.

With steely resolve, she declares that she will never abandon her faith, no matter what horrors she may face in hell.

The demon knight's laughter fades as it realizes the woman's unwavering resolve, and it recoils slightly from her fierce demeanor. Despite its attempts to sow doubt and despair, the woman's faith shines brightly, a beacon of hope in the midst of despair. And as she stands firm in her convictions, she inspires those around her to hold fast to their beliefs and resist the temptations of evil.

The woman's voice reverberates through the chamber, her words echoing with a divine certainty that fills the air with a sense of hope and determination. She stands tall, unyielding in her faith as she challenges the demon knight with her unwavering conviction.

She proclaims that there is indeed a God, a divine force of righteousness and justice, who reigns over all creation. She declares that this god is the Alpha and the Omega, the

Defiance

beginning and the end, the ultimate authority over all existence. And she boldly asserts that this god is not absent or indifferent but present among them, watching and waiting to unleash divine judgment upon the forces of darkness.

As she speaks, her words carry a power and conviction that cannot be denied, stirring the hearts of those around her with a renewed sense of faith and determination. And though the demon may scoff and mock, the woman's faith remains unshakable, a testament to the enduring strength of the human spirit in the face of evil.

In her defiance, the woman embodies the hope and resilience of all who refuse to surrender to despair, standing firm in the belief that light will triumph over darkness and that, even in the depths of hell, the presence of God shines brightly, illuminating the path to redemption and salvation.

The demon knight's words carry a chilling confidence, its voice dripping with malice and contempt for the woman's faith. It scoffs at the notion of any divine intervention, declaring that even the mightiest of gods would be powerless against the forces of hell that now walk the earth.

With twisted pleasure, the demon taunts the woman, daring her to call upon her savior to try and stop the relentless advance of darkness. It mocks the idea that any being, mortal or divine, could stand against the overwhelming power of hell, which it claims has endured for eternity and now seeks to spread its torment to all.

As it speaks, its words echo with a sinister certainty, instilling doubt and fear in the hearts of those who listen. And though the woman may cling to her faith with unwavering resolve, the demon knight's words serve as a grim reminder of the formidable enemy they face, one that knows no mercy and will stop at nothing to claim victory.

The demon's boastful declaration sends a shiver down the woman's spine, its words dripping with arrogance and defiance. With a menacing smirk it flaunts its power, claiming that even the Almighty God himself would be no match for it in battle.

Defiance

Its words hang in the air like a dark omen, a chilling reminder of the formidable foes they face and the dire consequences of their defiance. And as it commands the woman and her companions to follow it, its tone leaves no room for argument or hesitation.

With a heavy heart, the woman realizes the grim reality of their situation. They are but pawns in a cosmic struggle between light and darkness, caught in the clutches of an enemy whose power knows no bounds. And though she may cling to her faith with unwavering determination, she knows that the road ahead will be fraught with peril and despair.

***

Meanwhile, the three women stand united in their resolve, their bond strengthened by their shared faith and determination. They cast aside the false promises of comfort and luxury offered by the demons of hell. With steely determination, they refuse to succumb to the temptations that surround them, clinging instead to the hope that their faith will deliver them from the clutches of darkness.

Their actions speak volumes, a defiant gesture against the tyranny of evil and a testament to their unwavering commitment to their beliefs. And though they may face unimaginable trials and tribulations in the days to come, they stand firm in their conviction that their faith will guide them through the darkest of times.

Together they wash away the stains of temptation, cleansing their bodies and souls of the taint of hell's influence. And as they stand side by side, their spirits unbroken and their resolve unyielding, they know they will emerge victorious in the end, their faith shining like a beacon of hope when there is only darkness.

A woman asks them why they do not bathe in the waters. Her question hangs in the air, met with a solemn gaze from the three women who stand apart from the rest.

Defiance

The tallest among them steps forward, her voice steady and resolute as she addresses the curious woman's inquiry.

"We refuse to be swayed by the false promises of comfort and luxury these demons offer," she explains, her words carrying the weight of conviction. "We will not be complicit in their schemes, nor will we sacrifice our dignity and integrity for their twisted desires."

She looks around at the other women, her gaze unwavering. "We choose to stand firm in our faith and principles, even in the face of temptation and adversity. We will not betray ourselves or our beliefs, no matter the cost."

Her words resonate with the other two women, who nod in agreement. Together they stand united against the forces of darkness, unwavering in their resolve to resist the temptations of hell and remain true to themselves. And though their path may be fraught with peril, they face the future with courage and determination, trusting in the strength of their convictions to guide them through the trials ahead.

The woman's counterargument echoes through the chamber, piercing the tense atmosphere with her fervor. The three steadfast women exchange glances, unmoved by her impassioned plea. With quiet resolve, the tallest among them steps forward once more, her voice calm yet firm.

"We understand your perspective, but we cannot compromise our principles for the sake of false honor or empty promises," she says, her tone unwavering. "We refuse to be complicit in the atrocities committed by these demons, regardless of the consequences."

She looks around at the other women, her gaze unwavering. "We choose to hold fast to our integrity and morality, even in the face of adversity. We will not sacrifice our souls for the sake of fleeting glory or temporary comfort."

Her words hang in the air, a solemn reminder of the importance of staying true to one's beliefs, even in the darkest of times. And though the path ahead may be fraught with peril, these three women stand united in their defiance, resolute in their commitment to uphold what is right and just, no matter the cost.

The other women nod in agreement, their eyes reflecting determination and resilience. They understand the significance of their connection to the earth and the responsibility they bear to protect it from the forces of darkness.

"We must stand together as guardians of this planet," one of them says, her voice filled with conviction. "Our bond with the earth runs deep, and we cannot allow it to be tarnished by the evil intentions of those who seek to exploit and destroy."

"We may face challenges and sacrifices along the way," another adds, "but our commitment to preserving the beauty and sanctity of this world is unwavering. We will fight for what is right—for ourselves, for future generations, and for the earth itself."

With renewed resolve, the women gather their strength, ready to face whatever trials may come their way as they stand united in their determination to protect the planet they call home.

***

As the women follow the demon knight toward their designated quarters, they exchange nervous glances, trying to maintain a facade of composure despite the uncertainty and fear lurking within them. They whisper words of encouragement to each other, reminding themselves of their shared determination to resist the evil that seeks to consume them.

Upon reaching their destination, they enter a room bathed in the eerie glow of the red ruby light. The furnishings are opulent yet sinister, reflecting the dark nature of their surroundings. The women quickly find garments laid out for them, made of luxurious fabrics that seem to shimmer with an otherworldly sheen.

Defiance

Despite their trepidation, they don the garments, adjusting them with trembling hands as they prepare to face whatever awaits them in the service of their malevolent masters. With each garment they slip on they feel a weight of resignation settle upon them, but they refuse to let it extinguish the flicker of defiance burning within their hearts.

As they stand together in their newfound attire, they share a silent vow to remain strong in the face of adversity, united in their determination to resist the darkness. With resolve in their eyes, they await whatever trials may come, ready to confront them with courage and resilience.

***

A woman recoils at the touch of a demon knight, her instincts screaming at her to resist its advances. With a defiant glare, she wrenches herself free from its grasp, her eyes ablaze with determination.

"I will never give myself to the likes of you," she declares, her voice ringing with defiance. "My soul belongs to a higher power, one that you could never hope to comprehend. No matter what you do, you will never break me."

Her words hang in the air, a challenge to the demon's authority and a testament to her unwavering resolve.

Despite the fear coursing through her veins, she stands tall, refusing to succumb to the all-consuming darkness.

The demon knight's eyes narrow in frustration, but it knows better than to push further in the face of such fierce defiance. With a hiss of frustration, it releases her, allowing her to join the other women as they continue their journey through the depths of hell.

Though her heart may be heavy with fear, the woman remains steadfast in her conviction, ready to face whatever trials may come as she fights to preserve her soul and resist the forces of evil that seek to claim it.

As the woman joins the others, her mind races with thoughts of the demon's proposition and the implications of its desire.

Defiance

She feels a shiver run down her spine at the memory of its touch, its gaze burning into her with an intensity she cannot shake.

Despite her fear and uncertainty, she knows she cannot let herself be swayed by the temptations of the demon knight. She clings to her inner strength, drawing upon her faith and resolve to resist the darkness that surrounds her.

 As they continue their journey through the depths of hell the woman remains vigilant, her senses alert for any sign of danger or deception. She knows that they face unbearable challenges ahead, but she refuses to give in to despair.

With each step she reaffirms her commitment to fight for her freedom and the salvation of her soul. Though the path ahead may be fraught with peril, she knows that if she holds fast to her faith and her courage, she will find a way to overcome the darkness that threatens to consume her. The woman ignores the demon's threats, her resolve unshaken by its words. She knows she must stay strong and focused, trusting in the power of her faith to guide her through the trials ahead. As she reunites with her companions, they exchange determined glances, silently affirming their shared commitment to resist the forces of darkness that seek to enslave them. Together they will face whatever challenges come their way, drawing strength from their bond and their unwavering belief in a higher power.

As they are taken to their new quarters, the woman's thoughts are bolstered by hopes of escape and freedom.

She knows their journey will not be easy, but she refuses to give up hope. With each passing moment she grows more determined to defy the demons that seek to break her spirit and reclaim her freedom, no matter the cost.

***

As the demon approaches Babylon, it takes in the scent emanating from the dragon with relish, finding it satisfying to its demonic senses. The demon knight knows that Babylon is

Defiance

a formidable guardian of the realm of hell, and it respects the dragon's authority and power.

Babylon, sensing the presence of the demon, raises his massive head and fixes his fiery gaze upon the approaching figure. He acknowledges the demon knight with a nod, indicating that it may speak.

The demon delivers its report to Babylon, informing him of the women who have been prepared to serve their new masters. It describes the lavish clothes and feast that await them, emphasizing the significance of these gifts in binding the women to the service of hell.

Babylon listens intently, his keen intellect processing the information provided by the demon knight. He understands the importance of ensuring the loyalty of the women who have been selected, knowing they will play a crucial role in the dark designs of their infernal overlords.

With a deep growl, Babylon acknowledges the demon's report, signaling his approval of the plan. He knows that the women will soon be fully indoctrinated into the service of hell, their wills bent to the whims of their demonic masters. As the demon knight departs, Babylon settles back into his position of vigilance, his powerful presence serving as a constant reminder of the dominion of hell over the earth.

The demon knight, satiated by the gruesome feast, acknowledges Babylon's approval with a bow before retreating into the depths of the throne room. As it walks away, its mind is brimming with the satisfaction of having pleased its master and furthering the dark agenda of hell on Earth.

Babylon, his massive form illuminated by the flickering flames of the feast, remains vigilant, his mind already plotting the next steps in the grand design of their infernal overlords. The scent of blood and flesh fills the air, a grim reminder of the dominance of hell over the realm of mortals.

***

Defiance

As the demon knight disappears Babylon's gaze lingers on the remnants of the feast, his thoughts shrouded in darkness and malice. The world outside may tremble at the sight of their coming, but within the halls of hell there is only the assurance of power and dominion.

With a mighty roar that echoes through the cavernous throne room, Babylon settles back into his position of watchfulness, his eyes ablaze with the fire of hell itself. The night is far from over and the forces of darkness are ever vigilant, ready to unleash their wrath upon the unsuspecting world.

Babylon takes flight, his massive wings casting shadows over the desolate landscape, And the demon knights bow their heads in obedience, acknowledging their orders to maintain order within the throne room. The two hellhounds, their fiery eyes glinting with malevolence, slink into the depths of the throne, ensuring that no one dares disturb the proceedings.

Meanwhile, in the swirling depths of hell, Lucifer, the master of darkness, awaits the arrival of his loyal servant.

The air crackles with anticipation as Babylon descends into the infernal abyss, his form illuminated by the fiery glow of the underworld.

With a resounding roar Babylon flies to his master. The time has come to enact their dark designs upon the mortal realm, and Babylon is ready to execute his master's will without question.

As Babylon navigates the fiery tunnel, the cacophony of screams and tortured souls echoes around him, a haunting symphony of despair. The hands and faces of the doomed reach out, grasping desperately for any semblance of freedom, but Babylon presses on, unmoved by their pleas. The tunnel twists and turns, leading deeper into the bowels of hell, where the darkness reigns supreme. Babylon's wings beat against the searing air, carrying him ever closer to his master, Lucifer, the embodiment of evil itself.

Finally, the tunnel opens into a vast cavern, illuminated by the flickering flames of a thousand infernos. In the center of

Defiance

it all, seated upon a throne of bones and shadows, sits Lucifer, his eyes burning with a malevolent glow.

Babylon approaches his master, bowing low before him, a sign of reverence and submission. Lucifer regards his loyal servant with a knowing smile, acknowledging the role he has played in their dark designs.

Together, they discuss their plans for the mortal realm, weaving a tapestry of chaos and destruction that will consume all who oppose them. As they speak, the souls of the accursed swirl around them, their anguished cries serving as a grim reminder of the power they wield.

With their plans set in motion, Babylon prepares to return to the surface, his heart filled with a sense of purpose. The world above will soon feel the full force of their wrath, and none shall escape the darkness that they unleash.

As Babylon takes flight once more, the screams of the suffering fade into the distance, drowned out by the roar of flames and the promise of eternal suffering. For in the depths of hell, there is no mercy, only darkness and despair.

As Babylon finds himself in a vast chasm adorned with glittering jewels and trophies of creatures from realms beyond imagination. But instead of marveling at the spectacle before him, Babylon's eyes reflect a deep sense of revulsion and disdain.

The creatures that populate this otherworldly realm are tortuous and grotesque, bearing little resemblance to the beauty and purity of life as it was intended to be. Each one embodies the very essence of evil, a stark contrast to the divine creations of the celestial realms.

Babylon knows that these abominations are the work of his master, Lucifer, the architect of darkness and corruption. With every step he takes he feels the weight of their malevolent presence pressing down upon him, a reminder of the insidious power that lurks within the depths of hell.

Despite the opulent surroundings, Babylon cannot shake the feeling of unease that grips him. This is not a place of beauty or wonder, but a twisted reflection of everything that is wrong with the world.

With a heavy heart, Babylon turns his gaze away from the horrors that surround him, steeling himself for the task that lies ahead. He knows he must serve his master, no matter the cost.

Babylon bows his head respectfully, acknowledging his master's authority. Lucifer, the embodiment of darkness and deceit, looks upon Babylon with cold, calculating eyes. Babylon's plea for assistance in dealing with the obstacles that stand in their way is greeted with a mixture of amusement and annoyance from Lucifer. The devil sees Babylon's pitiful expression and senses his reluctance to conduct the task at hand.

With a cruel smile, Lucifer grants Babylon's request, but not without a warning. He reminds Babylon of the consequences of failure, of the eternal torment that awaits those who dare to defy him.

Babylon nods obediently, understanding the gravity of his master's words. He knows that failure is not an option, that he must do whatever it takes to fulfill Lucifer's wishes and maintain his favor.

Babylon turns to leave, accompanied by the two arch demon knights Lucifer has assigned to him. He prepares himself for the challenges that lie ahead, knowing that the fate of both heaven and Earth hangs in the balance.

Lucifer's rage burns hot as he confronts Babylon's apparent negligence. He grips the dragon's head fiercely, his eyes ablaze with fury as he berates Babylon for his failure to eliminate the human flying machines.

Babylon bows his head in shame, feeling the weight of his master's wrath. He tries to explain his reasons for not intervening directly, emphasizing his enjoyment of the battle and the thrill of watching the warriors clash.

Lucifer is unmoved by Babylon's excuses. He sees only weakness and incompetence in his servant's actions, viewing them as a betrayal of their cause. With a cruel twist of his

Defiance

hand, Lucifer inflicts pain upon Babylon, reminding him of the consequences of his failure.

Babylon grits his teeth against the agony, his loyalty to his master bedeviled to its limits. He knows he must redeem himself in Lucifer's eyes, no matter the cost. With a steely resolve, Babylon swears to rectify his mistake and prove himself worthy of Lucifer's trust once more.

As Lucifer releases his grip on Babylon's head, the dragon's resolve hardens. He knows that the battle is far from over, and he will do whatever it takes to ensure that hell's dominance over Earth is entrenched for all eternity.

Babylon listens intently to Lucifer's words, his immense form quivering slightly with fear and anticipation. He acknowledges his master's commands with a deep bow of his head, promising to fulfill his duty and not disappoint Lucifer again.

As he turns to leave, Lucifer's voice stops him, reminding him of the task at hand. Babylon nods obediently, his seven heads bowing in deference to his master's authority. He assures Lucifer that he will retrieve Berserker, the chosen arch demon, and ensure that the problem is swiftly dealt with. With a final word of gratitude, Babylon takes his leave, his massive form disappearing into the shadows of hell's fiery depths. He knows that failure is not an option, the consequences of disappointing Lucifer too dire to contemplate.

As he sets out on his mission, Babylon's mind rages with determination and resolve. He will not rest until the problem is eradicated and the will of Lucifer is once again fulfilled.

***

Berserker rises from his kneeling position, his eyes glowing with anticipation as he listens to Babylon's words. He nods in understanding, his massive form radiating power and ferocity. With a deep growl of excitement, Berserker flexes his muscles, preparing himself for the coming battle.

Defiance

Babylon looks upon Berserker with approval, knowing he has chosen wisely for this task. The arch demon knight is known for his brutality and skill in combat, qualities that will be invaluable in dealing with the problem Lucifer has tasked them with.

Together, Babylon and Berserker make their way out of the feasting hall, their footsteps echoing through the dark corridors of hell. As they journey toward their destination the air crackles with tension and anticipation, for they both know they are about to face a formidable enemy.

With every step Babylon and Berserker draw closer to their goal, their minds focused on the task at hand. They may be servants of hell, but they are also warriors, ready to do whatever it takes to fulfill their master's will.

Babylon watches Berserker with a mixture of admiration and anticipation, knowing that the arch demon knight is eager for the coming battle. He nods in approval as Berserker equips himself with his formidable axe, his eyes gleaming with excitement at the prospect of unleashing havoc upon their enemies.

With Berserker by his side, Babylon spreads his own massive wings and takes to the air once more, the flames of hell trailing behind them as they soar through the fiery tunnel. As they approach the opening that leads back to Earth, Babylon's senses sharpen in anticipation of the battle to come.

The two demonic warriors emerged from the tunnel, their eyes scanning the skies for any sign of the flying machines that have proven to be a thorn in their side. With their weapons at the ready and their minds focused on the task ahead, Babylon and Berserker prepare to face their enemies head-on, determined to prove their strength and dominance over all who dare to oppose them.

As Babylon and Berserker descend upon the earth, their presence strikes fear into the hearts of the starving people gathered below. Babylon's booming voice echoes through the air, announcing Berserker as the harbinger of destruction,

Defiance

the Omega who will bring an end to those who dare to oppose Lucifer, the dark lord of hell.

The people look up in horror and disbelief, realizing they stand in the presence of true evil incarnate. People fall to their knees in despair, while others scramble to flee, knowing that they are powerless against the might of Babylon and Berserker.

Berserker stands tall and imposing, his eyes burning with a fierce determination as he prepares to unleash his fury upon the unsuspecting mortals. With his axe held high, he waits for Babylon's command, ready to administrate the will of their master with ruthless efficiency.

Babylon watches the chaos unfold below, a wicked grin spreading across his monstrous face. The time has come for them to assert their dominance over the earth, and woe betide any who stand in their way.

***

As Berserker enters the throne of Lucifer the hellhounds obediently follow, their hot tongues licking at his face with a fervor that would terrify any mortal. But Berserker welcomes their presence, knowing their loyalty to their master is unwavering.

Inside the throne room the air is thick with an oppressive darkness, and the walls seem to pulse with malevolent energy. Berserker strides confidently forward, his axe held at the ready, prepared to conduct whatever task Lucifer has set before him.

As they reach the feeding room, Berserker's eyes gleam with anticipation at the sight of the lavish feast laid out before them. He wastes no time tearing into the meaty offerings, devouring them with an insatiable hunger that knows no bounds.

The hellhounds, too, join in the feast, their jaws snapping eagerly at the succulent flesh. Together they feast in gluttonous abandon, relishing the taste of their prey and the power it gives them.

But even as they indulge in their feast, a sense of foreboding hangs in the air. For they know that their actions serve only to further the dark agenda of their master, Lucifer, and that they are but pawns in his eternal game of domination and control.

As Berserker indulges in the sumptuous feast laid out before him, the women seated at the table cast fearful glances in his direction, knowing the fate that awaits them in the clutches of the arch demon knight. Dozens of them tremble in terror, while others try to maintain a facade of composure, knowing that any sign of weakness could spell their doom.

Berserker, oblivious to their fear, devours the food with ravenous hunger, his eyes gleaming with satisfaction as he relishes the flavors of the underworld. His fury hounds from hell sit obediently by his side, their tongues lolling out as they eagerly await their next command.

Meanwhile, the demon knights that roam the throne room keep a wary distance from Berserker and his companions, recognizing the danger he poses. They know better than to provoke the wrath of the arch demon knight, lest they incur his fiery fury.

As Berserker continues to feast, the women seated around him exchange fearful whispers, wondering what fate awaits them at the hands of this fearsome creature. But amidst their terror a glimmer of hope remains as they cling to the belief that someday, somehow, they will find a way to escape the clutches of hell and return to the world above.

The lost souls, trembling in fear at Berserker's threatening demeanor, quickly scurry to fulfill his demands. They rush to prepare a separate dish for the arch demon, hoping to appease his insatiable appetite and avoid his wrath.

Meanwhile, the women seated at the table exchange fearful glances, their hearts pounding with dread at Berserker's menacing words. They know that they are powerless to resist

Defiance

the will of the demons that now rule over them; they can only
pray for deliverance from the torment that awaits them.
As the lost souls hurry to prepare Berserker's meal, the
atmosphere in the throne room grows increasingly tense, with
the arch demon knight's fury casting a shadow of fear over
all present. It is a stark reminder of the cruel reality of life in
hell, where the strong prey upon the weak and mercy is a rare
and fleeting commodity. As Berserker indulges in the raw
meat, the women at the table exchange horrified looks, their
fear deepening at the sight of the arch demon's gruesome
appetite. They shrink back in their seats, praying silently for
deliverance from the horrors of hell.
The lost souls, sensing Berserker's satisfaction with the
appetizer, feel relieved, grateful they have managed to
appease the fearsome demon for the time being. They retreat
to the shadows, hoping to avoid any further confrontation
with the terrifying creature.
Meanwhile Berserker continues to feast on the raw meat with
savage gusto, his eyes gleaming with malevolent satisfaction.
The scent of blood and death hangs heavy in the air, a grim
reminder of the brutality and cruelty that define life in the
depths of hell.
As the feast continues the women can only watch in silent
horror, knowing they have been trapped in a nightmare from
which there may be no escape. They cling to whatever shreds
of hope and courage they have left, praying for a miracle to
save them from the clutches of evil that now surround them.
The demon knight server sneers at the three defiant women,
its eyes flashing with annoyance at their refusal to comply
with its orders. It tries to assert its authority over them,
warning them of the consequences of disobedience in hell.
However, the three women stand their ground, their defiance
unwavering in the face of the demon's threats. They refuse to
be complicit in the evil that surrounds them, determined to
hold to their principles and integrity even in the darkest of
times.

Defiance

The other women at the table watch in awe and admiration as the three rebels boldly reject the offerings of hell, inspired by their courage and resolve. They may not have the same strength to defy their captors, but they silently pledge their support to the brave souls who dare to resist.

The demon knight, realizing it cannot force the women to eat, storms out of the room in frustration, leaving the rebels to their fate. Despite the uncertainty of their future, the three women remain steadfast in their belief. They will not be swayed by the temptations of evil, clinging to the hope of eventual liberation and salvation.

As the demon knight leaves, the three women who refuse to eat the offered meal feed the raw meat to the hellhounds in the room. Berserker suddenly roars out in laughter, startling all those present. The three women, relieved by Berserker's unexpected reaction, exchange glances of gratitude and relief. They continue to feed the hellhounds, feeling a sense of camaraderie with the creatures as they defy the expectations of their captors. The other women at the table watch in amazement, inspired by the courage and defiance of the rebels.

Berserker's laughter echoes through the room, breaking the tension and filling the space with a sense of defiance and rebellion. The demon knight's threat has been thwarted, and the women find a small victory in their act of resistance.

As Berserker continues to laugh the atmosphere in the room shifts, becoming lighter and more hopeful despite the darkness that surrounds them. The women, emboldened by their small triumph, exchange whispers of encouragement, strengthened in their resolve to resist the forces of evil that seek to oppress them.

Though their journey ahead is fraught with danger and uncertainty, the three women find solace in the bond they share and the knowledge that they are not alone in their fight against the darkness.

As the women obediently follow the demon knight back to their quarters, they exchange nervous glances, knowing they are leaving Berserker alone with his gruesome meal. Despite their fear, they feel a sense of relief at escaping the oppressive atmosphere of the dining hall.

Meanwhile, Berserker wastes no time digging into the grotesque feast before him. With each bite he revels in the taste of raw flesh, savoring the sensation of blood dripping down his chin. The lost souls scurry around, replenishing his plate with more macabre offerings, eager to appease the fearsome arch demon knight.

As Berserker continues his feast, a demon knight watches from a distance, wary of the unpredictable creature's volatile nature. He knows better than to disturb Berserker while he indulges in his meal, understanding the consequences of provoking such a powerful being.

Back in their quarters, the women try to push aside thoughts of the horrors they have witnessed, focusing instead on the slim hope of escape. They huddle together, drawing strength from each other as they prepare for whatever trials may lie ahead. Despite the darkness that surrounds them, they cling to the belief that their faith and determination will guide them to freedom.

As the women enter their rooms they are greeted by the sight of chilled wine bottles. They exchange puzzled glances, unsure of what to make of this unexpected offering. Despite their reservations, the allure of the wine proves too tempting to resist, and they eagerly begin to indulge, savoring the sweet taste as it washes away the bitter memories of the evening's events.

Meanwhile, Berserker continues his savage feast, tearing into the gruesome spread with ferocious abandon. The two hounds from hell, enticed by the scent of fresh food, heed the demon knight's call and hurry off to claim their share, leaving Berserker to feast alone in the dimly lit dining hall.

As the night wears on and the wine flows freely, the women find themselves succumbing to its intoxicating effects, their worries and fears momentarily forgotten in the haze of alcohol. They laugh and chat amongst themselves, finding solace in each other's company as they cling to the hope of a brighter tomorrow.

In the dining hall, Berserker shows no signs of slowing down, his insatiable hunger driving him to devour every morsel of flesh before him. The demon knight watches from a distance, its grin widening as it anticipates the chaos sure to follow in the wake of Berserker's insatiable appetite.

As the women continue to drink the cursed wine, unaware of its diabolical origins, their laughter grows louder and their inhibitions fade away. They revel in the euphoria of the moment, blissfully unaware of the dark fate that awaits them. Meanwhile, the three women who have abstained from partaking in the wine's intoxicating allure watch on with growing concern. They exchange worried glances, realizing the true nature of the drink they have been offered. With each sip they fear that their fellow women are sealing their own doom, unwittingly surrendering themselves to the clutches of hell.

As the night wears on and the effects of the cursed wine take hold, the women who have indulged become increasingly oblivious to their surroundings. Their laughter turns to slurred speech, their movements sluggish and uncoordinated as they succumb to the intoxicating influence of the devil's blood.

In their corner the three sober women cling to each other, resolved to resist the temptations that surround them. They pray for strength and protection, determined to escape the sinister fate that awaits those who have fallen under the sway of hell's influence. With each passing moment their resolve strengthens, their faith their only shield against the encroaching darkness.

Indeed, the fate of those who have indulged in the cursed wine from hell hangs in the balance, their souls teetering on the edge of eternal damnation. As they revel in their drunken stupor, unaware of the dire consequences of their actions, the three women who resisted temptation remain steadfast in their resolve.

Defiance

Their faith and determination may be the only hope they have against the darkness. But as the night unfolds and the forces of evil close in around them, they must remain vigilant, ready to face whatever trials come their way, praying the strength of their convictions guides them through the perilous journey ahead.

The demon knight's satisfaction with the women's state of inebriation only serves to further solidify the grip of darkness over their souls. With their defenses weakened by the cursed blood wine, they are now more susceptible to the will of the demon lords.

The news of their readiness to serve Lucifer and the lords of hell will surely be received with approval by Babylon, the great dragon. It signals another step toward the fulfillment of the dark plans that have been set in motion.

As the forces of evil gather and the fate of humanity hangs in the balance, the three women who resisted temptation stand as beacons of hope in the face of overwhelming darkness. Their resolve will need to be deliberate as they confront the horrors that await them in the depths of hell.

But with their faith unyielding and their spirits unbroken, they may yet find a way to defy the darkness and emerge victorious in the ultimate battle between good and evil.

***

Babylon's satisfaction is tempered with caution, knowing there are still those who resist the will of hell and its forces, including the flying machines and any others who dare to oppose them. The women trapped within the clutches of the throne may harbor hopes of escape, but Babylon is wary of their potential defiance.

As the forces of darkness continue to gather and the conflict between good and evil escalates, Babylon remains vigilant, prepared to confront any threats to the dominion of hell. The women's resilience in the face of temptation may pose a challenge, but Babylon is confident in his ability to enforce the will of his master, Lucifer, and ensure the success of their dark plans.

The demon knight, surprised to find the room empty save for the two hellhounds, quickly scans the area, searching for any sign of Berserker. With a sense of urgency it approaches the hellhounds, hoping they might have an inkling of where Berserker has gone.

The hellhounds, their bellies full and their loyalty to Berserker unwavering, turn their fiery gaze toward the demon knight. Sensing the urgency in its demeanor, they communicate with the demon through their intense stares, conveying that Berserker has left the room but is still within the vicinity.

Realizing that time is of the essence, the demon knight thanks the hellhounds for their assistance and swiftly exits the room, determined to locate Berserker and fulfill Babylon's command to stand guard against any who oppose Hell's army... and the Prince of Darkness.

The demon knight and the hellhounds locate Berserker. He is trying to have his way with one of the women. The two hellhounds spring into action, rushing toward Berserker with a ferocity that echoes through the throne room. Berserker, caught off guard by their sudden attack, roars in anger as the Hellhounds knock him off the woman.

His eyes blaze with fury as he struggles to his feet, ready to retaliate.

The demon knight steps forward, its voice stern and unwavering.

"Berserker," it says, its voice low and dangerous, "you have defied the direct orders of our master. Your actions are a disgrace to the army of hell and a direct insult to Babylon." Berserker, his eyes still fixed on the woman, growls but does not respond. The demon knight raises his hand, summoning a surge of dark energy that crackles around him. "You will leave this place now," it commands. "You will stand guard outside the throne as ordered. Fail again, and not even your strength will save you from the wrath of Babylon and Lucifer."

With a snarl, Berserker finally tears his gaze away from the woman and storms out of the room. The demon knight watches him go, its expression is one of grim determination. It turns to the woman, who has become visibly shaken up, and speaks more softly. "Do not fear. You are under the protection of our master. Follow the rules and you will remain safe."

It then addresses the other demon knights in the room. "Return to your posts. Ensure that no further disturbances occur. Our master's plans must not be jeopardized."

As the demon knights disperse, the demon knight escorts the women to their quarters, ensuring they are secure and unmolested. The skies outside the throne remain dark and ominous, a reminder of the constant threat that looms over the world.

But with Berserker now standing guard, any who dares to challenge Hell's dominion will face a formidable adversary. The demon knight, satisfied that order has been reclaimed, turns its attention to the preparations for the next phase of their master's plan. The rebellion of the mortals and their flying machines must be crushed, and the dominance of hell must be assured of its victory. With a final glance at the now-quiet room, he exits, ready to report to Babylon and ensure that all is proceeding according to plan.

***

Berserker's powerful wings beat furiously as he ascends through the hole he created in the roof, pieces of the structure falling away like rain. His rage propels him forward and he lands outside the throne with a resounding crash, the ground shaking beneath his feet.

Babylon, the mighty dragon, awaits him with an expectant gaze, all seven heads watching intently. The air is thick with the scent of brimstone and the cries of tormented souls.

Defiance

"Berserker," Babylon rumbles, his voice echoing through the desolate landscape. "You are to stand guard here and ensure that no one, human or otherwise, interferes with our plans. The mortals with their flying machines have proven to be a nuisance, and I trust you to eliminate any threats with your... enthusiasm."

Berserker snarls, his anger still simmering beneath the surface. "As you command, Babylon. None shall pass without facing my wrath."

Babylon's central head lowers to meet Berserker's gaze directly. "Do not forget your place, Berserker. You serve our master, Lucifer, and his will is absolute. Control your impulses, or you will face consequences more severe than you can imagine."

With a grudging nod, Berserker turns and strides to his post, his presence a terrifying silhouette against the burning sky. The two hellhounds slink out to join him, wary but obedient. As Berserker takes his position, he casts a final glance back at the throne, his eyes lingering on the shattered roof. His thoughts are a maelstrom of fury and anticipation. He relishes the thought of the battles to come, eager to unleash his full power on any who dares to challenge hell's dominion.

***

The demon knight, meanwhile, reports back to Babylon, its expression a mixture of satisfaction and caution. "The women are secured, and Berserker is in position. All proceeds according to Lucifer's plan."

Babylon nods, his satisfaction tempered by a deep-seated wariness. "Good. But remain vigilant. The mortals are resourceful, and their desperation makes them dangerous. We must crush their hope completely if we are to ensure our dominance."

With a final glance at the darkening horizon, Babylon turns his attention back to the throne. The battle for Earth's future

Defiance

is far from over, and the forces of hell must remain united if they are to achieve total victory.

Babylon's multiple heads stare down at the humbled Berserker, their eyes glowing with a malevolent light. The air around them crackles with tension as the arch demon knight, battered and shaken, kneels in the crater he created.

"See that you remember your place, Berserker," Babylon growls, each of his voices resonating with the weight of hell's authority. "You are a powerful warrior, but even you are expendable if you defy the will of Lucifer." Berserker's wings droop as he bows his head, a gesture of submission. "I understand, mighty Babylon. I exist only to serve Lucifer and execute his will upon the earth."

Babylon's central head nods, satisfied. "Good. Now, guard the throne as instructed. Let no mortal, no matter their strength or ingenuity, breach our defenses. The fate of our conquest depends on our vigilance."

As Berserker rises from his knees, he can feel the eyes of the dragon on him, a constant reminder of the consequences of defiance. He spreads his wings once more and takes to the sky, positioning himself at the perimeter of the throne's entrance. Below him, the charred landscape of a once-thriving world stretches out, now a domain of desolation and despair.

The two hellhounds scan the horizon for any sign of intruders. The atmosphere is tense, each of them aware that the slightest misstep could lead to severe punishment—or worse.

As the sun sets, casting a blood-red hue over the sky, the forces of hell remain ever vigilant. Inside the throne the women, now bound to their fates, huddle together, the effects of the cursed wine beginning to take hold. Outside, Berserker and his hellhounds stand ready, their senses heightened, prepared to defend their master's dominion against any who dare challenge it.

The world above, though seemingly silent, brims with unseen defiance. Somewhere in the darkness, the remaining humans

Defiance

prepare for a fight that seems insurmountable, driven by a hope that refuses to be extinguished. And so the stage is set for the next clash in the ongoing battle between the forces of hell and the remnants of humanity.

Babylon, with his seven heads observing the horizon, lets out a deep, rumbling chuckle that reverberates through the desolate land.

Look there, Berserker," he points one massive claw toward the distant sky where faint lights flicker—a sign of the flying machines and their human pilots preparing to challenge the forces of hell.

"Those mortals in their machines think they can reclaim what is lost. Show them the folly of their defiance. Tear their machines from the sky and crush their spirits," Babylon commands, his voice dripping with contempt for the humans.

Berserker's eyes glow with a savage light as he follows Babylon's gaze. He flexes his wings and prepares to take flight, his muscles tense with anticipation. "As you command, Great Dragon. I will reduce them to nothing but ash and ruin."

With a powerful leap, Berserker launches himself into the sky, his wings beating furiously as he gains altitude. Below, the hellhounds growl and snap at the air, eager to join the fray but knowing their place is to guard the throne's perimeter.

As Berserker soars toward the approaching lights, the dark, bleeding sky seems to part before him, revealing the fragile human craft. He roars a challenge, a sound like a thousand thunderstorms, and dives toward the nearest target, his double-edged axe gleaming in the infernal light.

Inside the human aircraft, pilots steel themselves for the battle. They know the risks but hope and determination drive them forward. As they see the monstrous figure of Berserker approaching, they ready their weapons, knowing that this encounter could very well determine the fate of their world.

Berserker crashes into the first aircraft with terrifying force, his axe cleaving through metal and flesh alike. The human

Defiance

pilots fight back with everything they have, but they are no match for his fury. As he tears through the machines, their remnants falling from the sky like burning meteors, he feels the exhilaration of battle, the satisfaction of serving his dark master.

Back at the throne, Babylon watches with approval. "Yes, Berserker," he mutters to himself, "show them the power of hell. Crush their hopes and pave the way for our dominion." The battle rages on, with Berserker in the center of the chaos, a whirlwind of destruction. Each swing of his axe, each beat of his wings, brings humanity one step closer to despair. But in the hearts of the humans a flicker of defiance remains, a spark that refuses to die, no matter how dark the skies become.

As Berserker continues his assault, he remembers Babylon's words: after this, he can have any woman he desires. This thought fuels his rage, his desire for victory, and he fights with renewed vigor, determined to obliterate any threat to his master's reign and claim his reward.

Babylon, his immense form casting a shadow over the desolate landscape, turns his seven heads toward the horizon, each eye glinting with a malevolent gleam.

"Indeed, Berserker," he rumbles, his voice like the grinding of tectonic plates. "Their suffering will echo through the annals of hell, a testament to our power and their foolish defiance."

The Great Dragon's tails lash the ground, causing the earth to tremble once more, sending fissures spreading outward like dark veins. "Let them come," he snarls, "let them believe they have a chance. It will make their ultimate despair all the more delicious. "

Berserker, who has returned after his initial attack, his bloodlust barely contained, nods eagerly. "I will relish every moment, every scream. Their pain will be my symphony, and I will play it to perfection."

As they wait, the skies above churn with dark, brooding clouds, the air thick with the scent of brimstone. The captured humans below, huddled in their makeshift prisons, feel the oppressive weight of the demonic presence around them. They can sense the malevolent anticipation, the evil that looms just beyond their reach.

Babylon, his patience wearing thin but his resolve unyielding, addresses the imprisoned humans through a booming telepathic link. "Your would-be saviors will come, but their hope is a fragile thing, easily shattered. Watch as they fall, as you all will fall, into the abyss we have crafted for you."

The humans, despite their fear, cling to the slim hope that their rescuers will arrive. They whisper prayers, share stories of resistance, and hold onto the belief that light can pierce even the darkest night.

Meanwhile, the families and fighters preparing to face Babylon and his horde make their final adjustments, steeling themselves for the imminent confrontation. They know the odds are against them, but their determination burns brightly, a beacon of defiance against the encroaching darkness.

As time inches forward, the skies begin to fill with the distant hum of approaching aircraft. The humans' hearts beat faster, a mix of fear and hope, while the demons, led by Berserker and Babylon, prepare for the battle that will determine the fate of all souls.

Babylon, sensing the approach of the human forces, lets out a roar that shakes the heavens. "Now, Berserker! Let us welcome our guests. Show them the true meaning of terror!" With that, Berserker launches into the sky once more, his massive form cutting through the air with lethal grace.

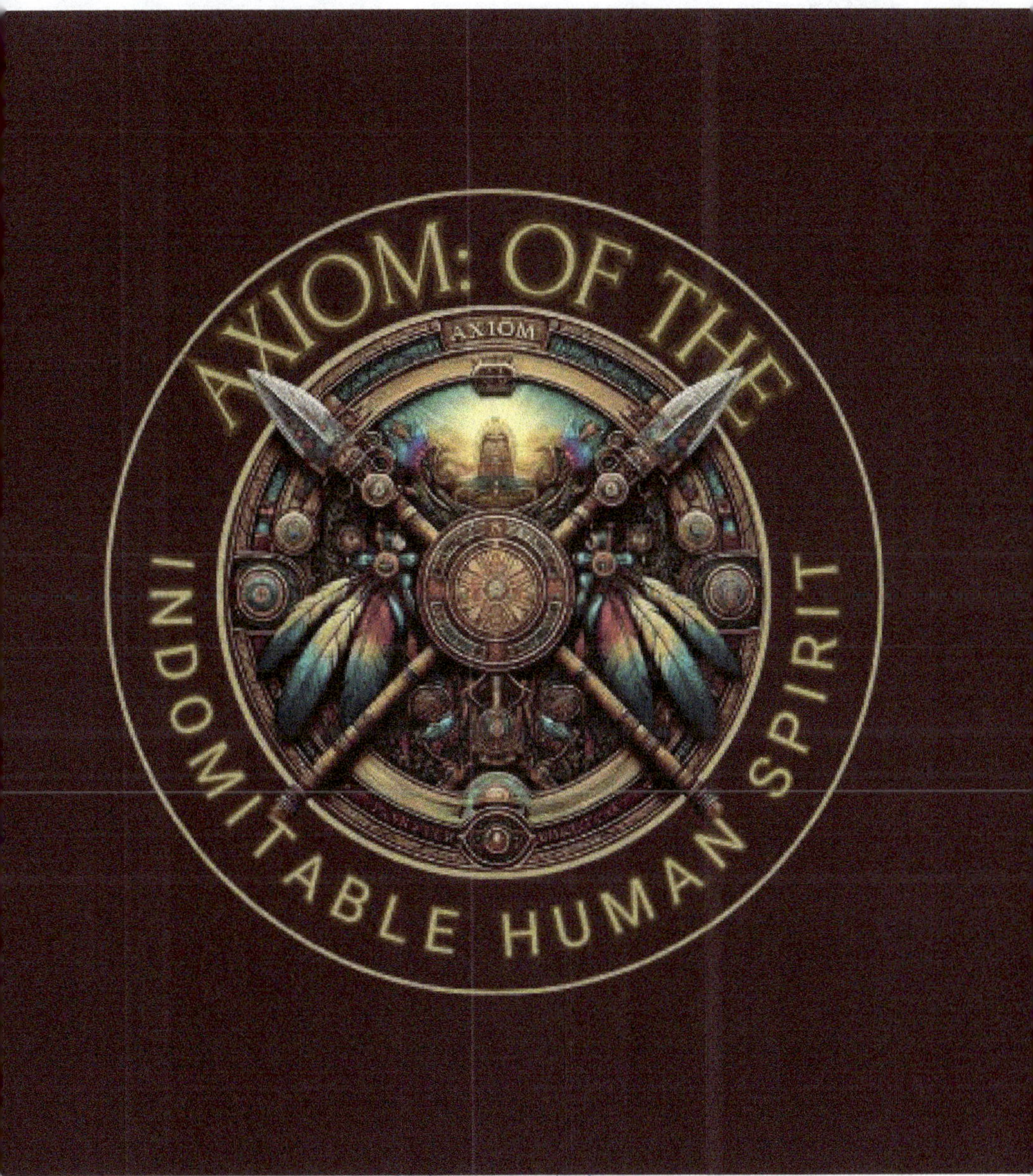
AXIOM: OF THE
INDOMITABLE HUMAN SPIRIT
AXIOM

CHAPTER: THREE
CLASH BETWEEN
HOPE and DESPAIR

Clash Between Hope and Despair

Below, the demons and hellhounds prepare to unleash their fury, the ground itself seeming to pulse with dark energy. As the human aircraft comes into view, their pilots see the looming figure of Berserker hurtling toward them, a harbinger of destruction. The battle is about to begin, a clash between hope and despair, light and darkness.

Babylon watches with a cruel smile, ready to savor every moment of the carnage. This time, he vows, there will be no mercy, no escape. Only the relentless, unyielding power of hell.

Babylon's seven heads remain fixed on the horizon, his myriad eyes never blinking, never wavering. His patience, a testament to his ancient and malevolent nature, contrasts with the restless energy of the arch demon knight beside him. Berserker's request breaks the heavy silence, his voice tinged with the hunger and anticipation that define his existence.

The Great Dragon shifts one of his heads to face Berserker directly, his eyes glowing with an inner fire. "Patience, Berserker," he rumbles, his voice reverberating through the ground like distant thunder. "The time for feasting will come, and it will be glorious. But for now, you must remain vigilant. The skies may seem calm, but treachery often hides in silence."

Babylon's gaze sweeps back to the horizon, a predatory gleam in his eyes. "Our master, Lucifer, demands unwavering loyalty and vigilance. We cannot afford to let our guard down. The mortals are cunning, and their defiance, though futile, can be unpredictable."

Berserker nods, his massive form trembling with barely contained energy. "As you command, great Babylon. I will remain here, ready to unleash hell upon those who dare to challenge us."

Babylon allows a slight nod of approval. "Good. Let your hunger fuel your vigilance. Let your rage sharpen your senses. When the time comes, you will have your fill of blood and carnage."

Clash Between Hope and Despair

The arch demon knight stands taller, his wings stretching and then folding back with a sense of renewed purpose. He gazes into the dark, bleeding skies, every fiber of his being attuned to any sign of movement, any hint of the approaching enemy. Hours continue to pass, the oppressive atmosphere growing heavier with each moment. The silence is thick, almost tangible, as if the very air is holding its breath in anticipation of the coming storm.

Then, as the horizon begins to glow with the dim light of a distant explosion, the faint hum of engines reaches their ears. Berserker's eyes narrow, his claws flexing in readiness.

"They are coming," he growls, a savage grin spreading across his face.

Babylon's heads all turn toward the approaching threat, his massive form coiling in preparation. "Indeed," he hisses, his voice filled with dark satisfaction. "Let them come. Let them witness the true power of hell. Berserker, you know what to do."

With a roar that shakes the very foundations of the earth, Berserker launches into the sky, his wings beating with the force of a hurricane. Below, Babylon's seven heads bellow in unison, a sound that echoes across the desolate landscape, a terrifying herald of the destruction to come.

The battle is imminent, the forces of hell prepared to unleash their fury upon the hapless mortals who dare to challenge their dominion. And at the forefront of this onslaught stands Berserker, the arch demon knight, ready to fulfill his dark purpose with savage glee.

Berserker moves through the kitchen with an air of ferocity, the lost souls scattering out of his way, terrified of his insatiable hunger and unpredictable wrath. He grabs chunks of raw, bloody meat from the counters, his hands dripping with the crimson remnants of his feast. He tears into the flesh with savage delight, relishing the taste of the fresh kill.

The kitchen is a macabre sight, with the remains of the deceased and mutilated animals being prepared for the unholy denizens of hell. Berserker pays no attention to the gruesome surroundings, his focus solely on satiating his voracious appetite. The lost souls, wretched and tormented, dare not meet his gaze as they continue their gruesome tasks, hoping to avoid his ire.

As he gorges himself, Berserker keeps a keen eye on the passing time, aware of the grave consequences if he fails to return to Babylon's side within the allotted half-hour. His mind is a whirl of primal urges and disciplined focus, a balancing act only an arch demon knight of his caliber can maintain.

When he is finally sated, Berserker wipes the blood from his mouth with the back of his hand and lets out a low, satisfied growl. He turns to leave the kitchen, shoving past the cowering lost souls with little regard for their plight. He knows he must return to Babylon, and he relishes the thought of the impending battle against the mortals who dare to defy hell's might.

Making his way back to the surface, Berserker spreads his wings and takes to the skies, flying with fierce determination. The half-hour is nearly up, and he has no intention of facing Babylon's wrath for tardiness. As he approaches the area where Babylon waits he can see the massive form of the great dragon, his seven heads scanning the horizon, ever vigilant for signs of the approaching enemy.

Berserker lands beside Babylon, his presence a mere shadow compared to the colossal dragon, but his aura of menace and power undeniable. "I have returned, Great Babylon," he announces, his voice a guttural snarl. "I am ready to do your bidding."

Babylon acknowledges Berserker's return with a slight nod from one of his heads. "Good," he rumbled. "The time for battle is upon us. Stand ready, for the mortals approach. We will show them the true power of Hell, and they will know despair."

Berserker, filled with renewed purpose and anticipation, turns his gaze to the dark, bleeding skies, ready to unleash his fury upon those who dare to oppose the will of Lucifer and the might of hell.

***

The ten state-of-the-art stealth mech fighters, having navigated the dark, foreboding skies, finally spot the remnants of the military auxiliary airport in Greensboro, North Carolina. The control tower's broken glass glints in the light from the fighters, acting as a beacon for the weary pilots. With precision and relief, they descend toward the runway, the stealthy hum of their engines barely audible over the eerie quiet of the desolate landscape.

The pilots, elite soldiers from a resistance force, are keenly aware of the dangers they face. They know they are the most wanted targets of Babylon and his terrifying warrior, Berserker. As they land they immediately begin the process of securing the area, aware that their presence might soon be discovered by the forces of hell.

The lead pilot, Captain Sarah Mitchell, exits her mech fighter and surveys the surroundings. The airport is in ruins, a stark reminder of the devastation that has befallen the earth. Despite the desolation, there is a sense of hope and determination among the pilots. They have found what they were searching for—a temporary sanctuary and a potential base of operations.

"Secure the perimeter and set up a defensive grid," Captain Mitchell orders, her voice firm and authoritative. "We need to be ready for any potential attacks. It won't take long for Babylon and Berserker to realize we're here."

The pilots spring into action, their training and discipline evident in their swift movements. They deploy advanced sensors and automated turrets, creating a defensive perimeter around the airport. Despite their exhaustion, they work with a sense of urgency, knowing that every second counts.

Inside the control tower, they establish a temporary command center. The equipment is old and battered, but they manage to get the main systems online. As they monitor the skies and surrounding areas, they cannot shake the feeling of being watched.

Meanwhile, high above, Babylon and Berserker continue to survey the skies. Babylon's multiple heads turn in unison, sensing a disturbance.

"They are here," Babylon rumbles, his voice echoing like thunder. "The mortals have landed. Prepare yourself, Berserker. Our prey has revealed themselves."

Berserker, with a savage grin, flexes his wings and claws. "They won't escape this time," he growls. "I will make sure of it."

***

Back at the airport, the tension is palpable. Captain Mitchell gathers her team. "We knew this moment would come. Babylon and Berserker will be upon us soon. Remember your training and stay focused. We are humanity's last hope. Let's show them what we're made of."

As the sun sets and darkness envelops the land, the resistance fighters brace themselves for the imminent confrontation. The air is thick with anticipation, and the stakes have never been higher. The battle for survival is about to begin, and the future of humanity hangs in the balance.

***

The night flares cast an eerie glow over the devastated landscape of the military auxiliary airport in Greensboro, North Carolina. The sight that greets the pilots is grim: a graveyard of twisted metal, shattered concrete, and decomposing bodies, remnants of the brutal thirty-year war that raged here. The airport, once a refuge, now stands as a haunting testament to the horrors of the past.

Eli, the seasoned leader and father of three skilled pilots, issues a crucial order to clear the runway. "Aim carefully.

Clash Between Hope and Despair

We cannot afford to miss," he commands, his voice steady despite the grim surroundings. The pilots understand the stakes; they need a safe landing before their fuel runs out. The stealth mech fighters, sleek and powerful, maneuver into position. They line up for a precision strike, their cannons primed and ready. The darkness, punctuated by the sporadic flare light, makes targeting the debris challenging, but these pilots are among the best.

Eli leads by example, his mech fighter taking the first shot. The tank killer cannon fires, the projectile streaking through the night and impacting a large chunk of the collapsed control tower. The explosion is controlled, reducing the rubble to manageable fragments without compromising the integrity of the runway. Encouraged by success, the other pilots follow suit.

Each fighter takes turns, systematically blasting the debris covering the runway. The precision of their shots is remarkable, a testament to their training and experience. Dust and fragments fill the air, but the runway slowly clears, becoming more navigable with each strike.

"Good job, everyone. Keep it up," Eli's voice crackles over the comms. "We're almost there."

With the final shots, the major obstacles are reduced to dust and manageable debris, revealing a clearer path for landing. The pilots, now confident in their ability to land safely, prepare for descent. The flares, though fading, provide just enough illumination to guide them in.

Eli's mech fighter is the first to touch down, landing smoothly on the cleared runway. One by one, the other fighters follow, their landings precise and efficient. The ground teams quickly mobilize, securing the area and setting up a perimeter around the airport.

The eerie silence of the night is broken only by the low hum of the mech fighters' engines winding down and the distant sounds of the forest. The air is thick with tension and the ever-present sense of danger.

Clash Between Hope and Despair

Eli gathers his sons and the rest of the team. "We've made it this far, but we can't let our guard down. Babylon and Berserker will be hunting us. We need to fortify this position and prepare for the worst."

The pilots, a mix of hardened veterans and determined new recruits, nod in agreement. They know the battles ahead will be fierce and unforgiving. They set to work, reinforcing their defenses, setting up automated turrets, and establishing a command center in the remnants of the control tower.

As the night deepens the flares burn out, leaving the airport bathed in darkness once more. The resistance fighters, however, are ready. They stand vigilant, their eyes scanning the horizon for any sign of Babylon and its hellish minions. Eli stands at the edge of the runway, looking up at the sky. He knows the fight for humanity's future is far from over and the greatest challenges are yet to come. But for now, they have a foothold, a chance to strike back against the forces of hell. And that is all they need.

The stealth mech fighters hover in formation, their high-intensity lights cutting through the red-tinged darkness that shrouds the planet. The pilots, each one highly skilled and trained for night operations, lock in their coordinates and prepare for a precise descent. The ground below is strewn with obstacles—debris, bodies, and remnants of structures—but they are determined to land safely.

Josias, a seasoned pilot and the son of Eli, takes point. His calm voice comes over the comms, giving final instructions to the squadron. "Stay at least a hundred feet behind each other. Maintain visual on the tail in front of you. Let's bring these birds down safely."

He leads by example, his mech fighter descending smoothly toward the cleared runway. The high-intensity lights illuminate the path, but the ground is still a treacherous landscape of ruins and the remains of war. Josias' hands are steady on the controls, his eyes focused on the landing zone. As Josias approaches the runway, he carefully maneuvers his fighter to avoid any last-minute obstacles. With practiced ease, he touches down, the mech's legs absorbing the impact as the craft comes to a halt on the blood-soaked ground. He immediately scans the surroundings, ensuring it is safe for the others to follow.

"Josias here. Landed safely. Follow my path and stay sharp," he instructs.

One by one the other mech fighters descend, each pilot maintaining the recommended distance. The red darkness and the lingering haze from the recent explosions make visibility a challenge, but the high-intensity lights provide just enough illumination. The pilots execute their landings with precision, the powerful legs of their mechs absorbing the impact as they touch down on the runway. The coordination is flawless, a testament to their rigorous training and experience.

Eli lands next, his fighter coming to a rest beside Josias. He steps out, his eyes scanning the perimeter as he gives a nod of approval to his son. "Good work, Josias. Let's get everyone down and set up a perimeter."

The rest of the squadron follows suit, each mech fighter landing without incident. The runway, once obstructed by debris, now serves as a secure landing zone for the resistance fighters. As the last mech fighter touches down, the pilots quickly exit their cockpits, ready to establish a defensive position.

 Eli takes charge, directing the team. "Secure the area. Set up automated turrets and sensors. We need to be ready for anything."

The team moves efficiently, setting up defenses and scanning the surroundings for any potential threats. The eerie silence of the night is punctuated by the hum of their equipment and the occasional crackle of their comms. The pilots, now on the ground, are acutely aware of the danger that lurks in the shadows.

As they work, the tension is palpable. They know Babylon and his forces will not be far behind. The mech fighters, now transformed into mobile command units, provide both a tactical advantage and a symbol of hope for the resistance.

Clash Between Hope and Despair

Josias, standing beside his father, looks up at the sky, the red hue a constant reminder of the hellish forces they are up against. "We did it, Dad. We're down, and we're ready."
Eli places a hand on his son's shoulder, a rare moment of tenderness amidst the chaos. "This is just the beginning, Josias. We have a long fight ahead of us. But together we'll make sure our sacrifice means something."
As the night deepens, the resistance fighters fortify their position. They are ready for whatever comes next, determined to reclaim their world from the grip of hell.
The presence of Babylon and Berserker looms large, but the fighters are resolute. They will face whatever horrors await, standing united in their quest to free humanity from darkness. Josias, leading the squad, maintains his focus, visualizing the intact airport he once knew. This mental image helps him guide his fighter and those following through the debris-laden darkness. Biggs, his brother, keeps vigilant watch from behind, ready to signal any adjustments needed for the formation.
As Josias touches down the mech's legs absorb the impact, sending a shower of sparks across the runway. He swiftly moves aside, giving the next fighter space to land. Each pilot follows suit, executing their landings with precision and speed, their training evident in every move. The runway lights up with sparks as the fighters skid to a halt one after another, each landing flawless despite the hazardous conditions.
Eli, watching from his landed position, feels a surge of pride and relief. "Excellent work, team. We made it. Now let's secure the area."
The pilots disembark from their fighters, their boots hitting the ground with purpose. They move swiftly, setting up a perimeter and deploying automated turrets and sensors to guard against any immediate threats. The hellish silence of the destroyed airport is disrupted only by the sounds of their preparations and the occasional crackle of their comms.

Clash Between Hope and Despair

Biggs, standing beside Josias, looks around the ruined landscape, his eyes filled with determination. "We did it, Josias. We're here. Now we just need to hold our ground." Josias nods, his eyes scanning the horizon.

Eli, stepping out of his fighter mech, exudes a determined energy. As he gears up, he speaks to the team, "We did well to get here, but our mission isn't over. We're going back to chop off the seven heads of the dragon called Babylon." His words ignite a spark of excitement and readiness among the team.

James approaches his father, sensing a lingering tension. "What's bothering you, Dad? We all got back safe."

Eli sighs, his expressions a mix of relief and frustration. "I'm grateful we made it back alive, but we didn't accomplish what we set out to do. I wanted to knock that dragon Babylon on his ass before we left."

James, with a fierce determination in his eyes, replies in a low tone, "We'll get our chance sooner than we think. We just need to be ready."

Father and son walk back to join the rest of the team, who are still on edge from the intense battle and treacherous landing. Despite the fatigue and the darkness that surrounds them, there is a palpable sense of camaraderie and shared purpose. They know they have achieved something significant by surviving and making it to this point.

As they take a moment to catch their bearings, the team begins to relax, their adrenaline gradually subsiding. They start to prepare for the next phase of their mission, confident in their abilities and motivated by the vision of their goal. The resolve to confront and defeat Babylon and his minions strengthens them.

Eli, feeling a renewed sense of determination, addresses the team. "Rest up, everyone. We've done well, but the real fight is still ahead of us. Stay sharp, stay ready. We'll take Babylon down and reclaim our world."

The team, inspired by Eli's words, settles into their temporary base, readying themselves for whatever comes next. The dark blood-red skies serve as a constant reminder of the battles they have fought and the ones yet to come. But with their spirits high and their purpose clear, they know they are prepared to face whatever hell throws at them.

***

Everyone looks around the airport in North Carolina, disgusted by the ugly, tormenting sight of the mutilated bodies that surround the airport, accompanied by the stench of a hundred morgues. If they had not been trained for times like this, they would have been sick to their stomachs long ago.

Mike speaks up, saying to everyone that they should gather up all the bodies, putting them in a certain spot and making a huge hole for a mass grave, giving the dead people a proper burial and praying for the murdered souls so they can rest at ease.

Mike's brother, Gage, is the first to agree, heading toward garbage trucks which are out of commission.

As Gage walks toward the garbage trucks, he turns around and asks the rest of them if they are going to help or if he is going to do it by himself, speaking with a tormented voice, clearly disgusted by the sight. They all immediately follow Gage to the garbage trucks, hoping they still work or can be repaired so they can put the bodies in the back and escort them to one of the fields outside the North Carolina airport. The first garbage truck they try is the only one still on four wheels. In the driver's seat is a corpse that looks as if he was seared from the inside out. Beside him in the passenger seat is another man, his head barely attached to his body and slumped over onto the dashboard.

Ethan grabs the burnt, decrepit body from the driver's seat, placing it outside the garbage truck, then jumps behind the wheel, finding the key still in the ignition. He turns the key, but nothing happens. Sarcastically, he asks the decapitated head on the dashboard if it knows what is wrong with the ignition. As Ethan continues to turn the key, he hears a voice saying, "If my head were on my shoulders, I'd be happy to help."

Ethan quickly turns to the maggot-infested head, his expression one of horror, convinced he is hallucinating. He goes to exit the garbage truck but the voice speaks again, telling him to get back in. Confused and scared, Ethan re-enters the truck, poking at the head and mushing the body, but nothing happens. When the voice tells him to turn the key again, Ethan, startled, kicks the body out of the truck, grabs the head, and tosses it with the body. He starts cursing, thinking he is losing his mind.

Just then, his friend Adonis steps out from the front of the truck, closing the hood, and yells at Ethan to turn the key and stop playing with the head and dead body. Ethan, eyes wide open, bursts into laughter, turns the key, and starts the truck. Jumping out, he mutters that he needs Tylenol.

Adonis, concerned, asks if Ethan is all right and suggests he rest while they collect all the remains if he needs it.

Ethan reassures Adonis that he was just imagining things but agrees they all need food, rest, and water. As if on cue, Adonis' stomach growls.

Adonis suggests that someone should search for any remaining supplies so they all can avoid dying from starvation.

Ethan and Adonis get back into the garbage truck and drive over to the rest of the team, who are working on three more trucks. Ethan stops in front of the garbage truck where Hunter and his brother, Charlie, are working. Adonis jumps out and asks Charlie to go with Ethan while he stays with Hunter to fix the garbage truck.

Charlie asks Ethan what they are supposed to do. Ethan explains that they need to check for food or water since everyone is ravenous. Charlie, holding his stomach, agrees and quickly rushes Ethan toward a facility that still appears intact. They both strap on their rifles and other small arms over their shoulders, preparing to find sustenance in the eerie quiet, leaving their mechs behind.

They carefully make their way inside the facility, eyes peeled for any signs of movement or hidden dangers. The inside of the building is dark and filled with shadows, but it appears structurally sound. As they move through the hallways, they come across a break room. Charlie whispers to Ethan, "If there's any food, it's probably in here."

They enter the break room cautiously, sweeping their rifles from side to side. The room is a mess, with overturned tables and chairs, but a vending machine and a small fridge catch their attention. Ethan pries open the vending machine door, finding stale but edible snacks inside. Charlie checks the fridge, discovering a crate with bottles of water and about twenty old, but still good, food cans.

"Jackpot," Charlie says, holding up the supplies. Ethan nods, stuffing the snacks into his pack. "Let's grab what we can and get back. Everyone will be relieved."

With their packs filled, they carefully make their way back to the team. As they approach, Ethan waves a hand to get Adonis' attention. "We found some food and water," he announces. Adonis and the others look visibly relieved as they gather around to share the supplies.

 With everyone a bit more energized and hydrated, they resume their efforts with renewed vigor. The grim task of clearing the bodies and fixing the trucks becomes a bit more bearable now that they know they have dwindling sustenance to keep them going. The team works in a more coordinated fashion, driven by the small victory of finding supplies amid chaos.

Hunter advises Ethan and Charlie to be careful and mentions to Adonis how thirsty and hungry he feels after their long flight. Ten minutes later, Adonis tells Hunter to get inside the garbage truck to try starting it up. Hunter sits in the driver's seat, closes his eyes, and turns the key, but nothing happens. Disappointed, he tries again, but still, nothing.

Clash Between Hope and Despair

Adonis then asks Hunter to give him a second while he repairs coordinated wires to their junctions, hoping his adjustments will be effective. He tells Hunter to try again. This time the garbage truck skips a couple of times before finally starting up, letting out a puff of black smoke.

Pollution is the least of their worries; their main problem is the demonic forces trying to unite and unleash hell on Earth, destroying everything in their path.

Celebrating their small victory, Adonis and Hunter give each other high fives. They jump into both garbage trucks and head toward a potential fuel source. They race the trucks, pushing the engines to ensure they will not break down from disuse.

As they drive, Hunter keeps an eye on the fuel gauge, hoping to find a tank of gas before running out. Adonis leads the way, navigating through the rubble and debris that litter the road. They head toward an old fuel depot on the outskirts of the airport, hoping the fuel is still able to pump through the lines and hasn't been looted or contaminated with particle debris.

When they arrive they find the depot in a state of disrepair, but the storage tanks appear intact. Adonis and Hunter quickly get to work, siphoning gas into the trucks. As they do, Hunter keeps watch, his eyes scanning the horizon for any signs of danger.

With the trucks refueled, they make their way back to the team. Hunter shouts over the engine noise to Adonis, "Let's hope these trucks hold up. We have tough work ahead of us."

Back at the base, Ethan and Charlie return with the food and water, distributing it to the grateful team members.

Everyone takes a moment to eat and drink, the small reprieve giving them a much-needed boost.

Adonis and Hunter park the refueled trucks next to the others, hoping out to join the rest of the team. "We've got the trucks running and some fuel," Adonis announces. "We should be good to start clearing the runway."

Clash Between Hope and Despair

With their spirits lifted and their bodies refreshed, the team resumes their work. They use the garbage trucks to clear debris, making space for their continued efforts against the forces of hell. Each task completed brings them one step closer to their goal, and they know they must stay focused and united to survive the battles ahead.

Everyone is pleased to hear about the fuel for the garbage trucks, but they also need jet fuel for the stealth fighters. Adonis goes to help Josias collect some wires from one of the engines. As soon as he looks at the engine, Adonis immediately tells Josias the way the wires look, with the engine thrown underneath the truck, it is as if something had attacked whoever was driving by crashing through the broken windshield. Josias looks at Adonis like he is crazy, then goes around to look inside the garbage truck for the first time, seeing a half-mutilated body laying across both seats.

Josias takes a good look at the torn body, noticing what looks like huge teeth marks from a shark or an oversized crocodile. He goes around, asking his brother to look at the body, then turns to his friend Adonis, asking what type of land animal could do such a thing. Adonis tells Josias he does not know, but if they take a wild guess, they will all probably say the same thing.

Adonis, Josias, and Biggs all look at the engine, then the windshield, finally leaving the body at the same time, saying in unison, "Hellhounds." Josias, curious, asks Adonis if he believes there are hellhounds still walking around.

Adonis tells Josias possibly, but they should have sniffed them out or heard them when they made all the noise before landing here. Biggs, Josias' older brother, chuckles and agrees with Adonis, telling Josias to calm down and not to worry, because if the hellhounds were still around Biggs would protect him anyway.

Ethan and Charlie, who had returned from their search for food and water with small cans and bottles they found in a nearby storage room, approach the others.

Clash Between Hope and Despair

Charlie notices the mutilated body and the conversation about the hellhounds. "If those things are still out here, we need to be on high alert," he says seriously.

Adonis nods. "We need to keep watch in shifts. We cannot afford to be off guard."

Hunter, overhearing the conversation, joins in. "We also need to find a way to get jet fuel for the fighters. If we need to make a quick escape or launch another attack, we cannot remain on the ground, we need to take to the skies.''

Eli steps forward, having overheard the plan. "There is a maintenance hangar on the far side of the airport. It might have what we need. Josias, Adonis, Biggs, and I will head there to check it out. The rest of you, stay here and keep getting the trucks and fighters ready.''

Everyone nods in agreement, understanding the urgency of their situation. Josias, Adonis, Biggs, and Eli gather their gear and head toward the maintenance hangar, weapons ready. The eerie silence of the airport is unsettling, but they press on, determined to find what they need to continue their fight against the forces of hell.

As they approach the hangar they move cautiously, scanning the area for any signs of danger. The hangar doors are slightly ajar, and Eli motions for the others to stay quiet as they slip inside. Within they find various tools and equipment scattered around, as well as a large fuel tank in the corner.

"Bingo," Adonis whispers, pointing to the tank.

Biggs and Josias start inspecting the tank, checking for any signs of damage or leaks. "It looks intact," Biggs says. "We should be able to siphon the fuel we need."

Eli keeps watch at the door while the others work quickly to set up a makeshift pump. They manage to get the fuel flowing into multiple containers, filling them up with as much as they can carry.

"We've got enough for now," Josias says, capping the last container. "Let's get this back to the others."

They carefully make their way back to the rest of the team, the weight of the fuel containers slowing their pace but not affecting their resolve. Reaching the team, they distribute the fuel, ensuring the stealth fighters are ready for whatever comes next.

Eli addresses the group, his voice firm. "We have what we need for now, but we cannot let our guard down. We will take turns keeping watch tonight. Rest when you can, because tomorrow we continue our mission."

The team nods in agreement, steeling themselves for the challenges ahead. United and prepared, they know their fight against the forces of hell is far from over.

Josias smiles but still feels cautious, wrapping his arm around Biggs. Biggs rubs his hair, telling Josias he will protect him. Adonis says they should get back to repairing the garbage truck so they can bury the decaying bodies.

Mike calls Josias, asking him to walk with him around the outside perimeter of the airport so they can try to find some more fuel for the jets and prepare their stealth mechs for flight.

Josias grabs his M50 rifle, throws it over his shoulder, then digs in his bag, grabbing a belt full of armor-piercing M50 tank killers, putting the belt around his other shoulder. He picks up an M16 with two extra clips holding fifty-two rounds each, saying, "You can never be too safe." Josias runs to Mike, telling him he is ready, then asks Mike what they would be looking for along with the fuel. Josias knows there is another agenda on Mike's mind.

Mike glances at Josias, a serious look on his face. "You're right, Josias. There's something else we need to discuss, but first let's find that fuel." They move cautiously around the perimeter, their eyes scanning the ruins for any signs of danger or hidden resources. The desolate landscape is eerily quiet, the remnants of the battle hauntingly still.

As they walk, Mike finally speaks. "Josias, I've been thinking about our next steps. We need to be strategic in our approach against Babylon. We cannot just rely on brute force; we need intelligence and a solid plan. We have to find out more about Babylon's operations, his weaknesses, and any potential allies we might have."

Josias nods, understanding the gravity of the situation. "I agree. We cannot afford any more surprises. But how do we gather that kind of information?"

Mike stops, looking at Josias intently. "There are rumors of the Aegis of Echoes operating nearby. They have been gathering intel on Babylon and his forces. If we can find them, we might be able to join forces and strengthen our position."

Josias processes this information, realizing the potential benefits of such an alliance. "Do you have any idea where to start looking?"

Mike pulls out a small map, pointing to a location not far away from the airport. "There's an old military outpost here. The US government abandoned it years ago, but the resistance might be using it as a base. We should check it out as soon as possible."

Josias agrees, feeling a renewed sense of purpose. They continue their search for fuel, eventually finding a stash hidden in an old maintenance shed. With even more fuel secured, they make their way back to the group, ready to share the new plan.

Back at the airport, the team is relieved to see them return with the much-needed fuel. Eli, seeing the determined looks on Josias and Mike's faces, asks, "What's the plan?"

Mike steps forward, explaining the situation to Eli and the rest of the team, then asking Eli if there is any chance they can contact Captain Sarah Mithchell and the Aegis of Echoes for a strategic coalition, Eli gestures with a finger pointing to his temple revealing to them all as soon as they can establish Comms again he will be able to link everyone together. The team listens intently, understanding the crucial imperative of the mission ahead. After the debriefing Eli nods approvingly. "It's a good plan. We'll split into two groups. One will continue fortifying our current position here and prepare the mechs for flights. The other will head out to the last outpost

Clash Between Hope and Despair

Captain Sarah Mitchell and the Aegis of Echoes were searching, which is not far from our present location, and establish a comms link in order to have her team continue their intelligence in real time while regrouping at the target destination… Manhattan."

Mike steps forward, explaining the situation to Eli and the rest of the team, then asking Eli if there is any chance they can contact the Aegis of Echoes and Captain Sarah Mitchell for a strategic coalition. Eli gestures, revealing to them all that as soon as they can establish comms again he will link everyone together. The team listens intently, understanding the high importance of the mission. After the debriefing, Eli nods approvingly. "It's a good plan. We'll split into two groups. One will continue fortifying our current position here and prepare the mechs for flight. The other will head out to the last outpost Captain Sarah Mitchell and the Aegis of Echoes were at, which is not too far from here, and establish a comms link at their facility in order to have them continue their intelligence in real time."

The team quickly organizes, ready to execute the plan. Josias, Mike, and the others gear up for the journey to the outpost, while Eli and the rest stay behind to secure the airport and prepare for any incoming threats.

As they set out, Josias feels a mix of excitement and apprehension. The stakes are high, but with a clear plan and a potential new ally, they have a fighting chance against Babylon. United and determined, they move forward, ready to face whatever challenges lie ahead.

Mike tells Josias he wants to check around and make sure nothing is still lurking, watching and waiting until they let their guards down before killing them off unexpectedly. Mike continues, saying he knows Josias feels the same way, so he figured the two of them would be more on point than the others. Josias agrees, quickly loading the chambers of his M16, and both make their way around the country airport. Meanwhile, Hunter and his cousin, Gage, are cleaning out the inside of the garbage truck's back. They wish they had soap and water but must deal with brooms they picked up from one of the garbage trucks. Eli, along with his son James, is cleaning out the rifles and counting the ammo left for each weapon. They are also ensuring the mech's artillery is well-kept, oiled, and ready to go. Eli tells James he knows of a military armory heavily guarded down the road about two miles from the airport. He suggests they go to the armory, hoping to find more ammo and more weapons if the armory is still standing. James agrees, telling his father they should check it out as soon as the trucks are prepared and ready to go.

***

Back outside, Mike and Josias continue their patrol, scanning the perimeter for any signs of movement. Josias keeps his grip tight on his M16, ready to fire at any threat.
They both know that letting their guard down, even for a moment, could be fatal. They pass by the wreckage that used to be an airport terminal, its once-bustling halls now silent and filled with shadows.
Mike pauses, motioning for Josias to stop. "Do you hear that?" he whispers. They both listen intently, straining to catch any sound over the rustling of the wind and the distant hum of the generators still running somewhere in the background. There is a faint noise, like scraping, coming from one of the hangars. They exchange glances and silently move toward the sound, ready for anything.
Inside the hangar, they find the source of the noise: a lone survivor, injured and weak, trying to make a signal fire out of the surrounding debris. The man looks up at them, his eyes filled with fear and relief. Mike and Josias quickly assess his condition, offering him water and basic first aid. They learn that he is a mechanic who managed to hide during the initial attack but was too injured to move far.
The survivor, whose name is Tom, tells them about a hidden cache of supplies nearby, including food, water, and medical

supplies. Grateful for the information, Mike and Josias help him to his feet, planning to bring him back to their camp for proper care. They also decide to check out the cache, hoping it will provide much-needed resources for their team.

***

Back at the camp, Eli and James are finalizing their plans for the armory raid. With the garbage trucks ready and the team beginning to regroup, they know time is of the essence. The fuel and supplies from the armory could make a significant difference in their fight against Babylon.
As night falls, the team gathers around a makeshift fire, sharing what little rations they have left. Despite the exhaustion and ever-present danger, there is a renewed sense of hope among them. They have a plan, resources are within reach, and the possibility of new allies gives them strength. Together, they are determined to face whatever comes next, united in their mission to take down Babylon and his evil forces.

***

Minutes go by, and Adonis finishes one of the garbage trucks that was already running. He calls Eli over to look and then suggests he and James go to the armory two miles down the road to get more ammo and weapons. Biggs asks his father, Eli, if he can go along with them. Eli tells him he needs to stay behind along with Adonis to help with the garbage trucks or whatever else might come along while they are gone. Adonis tells Biggs he would appreciate it if he stayed to help with the engines, so repairs are finished quicker. Biggs agrees, saying he does not mind; he just needed to know if they would need an extra gun just in case they bump into unexpected trouble they do not want.

Clash Between Hope and Despair

Both Eli and James grab ammo and rifles, throw them into the front of the garbage trucks, then jump in, ready to go check out the armory for the extra supplies they will need. They drive cautiously, their eyes scanning the desolate landscape, alert for any signs of danger. As they approach the armory, they see that the building is still standing, but the entrance is blocked by debris and a few burned-out vehicles. Eli and James get out of the truck, cautiously making their way to the entrance, rifles at the ready. They find a side entrance partially concealed by rubble and manage to squeeze through.

Inside, the armory is dark and eerily quiet. Eli motions for James to stay close as they navigate the narrow corridors. They find a storage room filled with crates of ammunition and weapons they desperately need. James starts loading up a crate while Eli keeps watch. Suddenly they hear a noise, a faint scraping sound, coming from deeper within the building. Both men freeze, listening intently.

James whispers, "Do you think it's one of those hellhounds?" Eli shakes his head, signaling for silence. They continue to listen, the sound growing louder. Eli grips his rifle tightly, preparing for whatever comes through the doorway.

The scraping stops, followed by a low growl. Eli motions for James to get behind him. As they wait, the growl intensifies, echoing through the narrow halls.

Suddenly a figure appears at the end of the hallway, shrouded in shadows. Eli raises his rifle, ready to fire, but the figure steps into the light, revealing itself to be a wounded soldier. The man stumbles forward, collapsing at their feet. Eli and James rush to his side, helping him up and quickly checking him for injuries.

The soldier, barely conscious, mutters about the attack and the monsters that came from nowhere. He points to a room deeper within the armory, saying there are more supplies and more survivors. Eli and James exchange a look, knowing they cannot leave anyone behind. They help the soldier to his feet, carefully making their way to the room he indicated.

Clash Between Hope and Despair

Inside, they find more supplies and more injured soldiers. Eli quickly assesses the situation, gathering all the supplies they can carry and helping the injured soldiers to their feet. They make their way back to the garbage truck, loading the supplies and injured soldiers into the back. Eli and James jump into the front, ready to head back to the airport. They will need to return for the weapons and ammunition.

***

Back at the airport, Adonis and Biggs finish repairing the last of the garbage trucks. They gather the rest of the team, organizing them for the task of collecting the bodies and giving them a proper burial. Ethan and Charlie join the others in the grim task.

As they work, they see the headlights of the returning garbage truck. Eli and James pull up, jumping out to help unload the supplies and tend to the injured soldiers.

Everyone is relieved to see the additional supplies, knowing they will need every bit of it for the battles to come.

With supplies from the armory and the repaired garbage trucks, the team feels a renewed sense of hope. They know the road ahead will be difficult, but they are determined to continue their fight against Babylon and his forces.

Together they will face whatever comes next, united in their mission to protect humanity and defeat the evil that threatens their world.

 Eli and his team are resolute. They know that to fight against the forces of hell means to face death and horror without fear. The demon knights and their hellish pets are fearsome adversaries, but the soldiers are determined not to let terror break their spirit. They know that hell is not just a physical place, but a manifestation of the evil born from human actions and thoughts. The battle between heaven, earth, and hell has raged since the dawn of time, fueled by the jealousy and greed of fallen angels like Lucifer.

Clash Between Hope and Despair

Lucifer, once the most beautiful of all angels, fell from grace because of his jealousy toward humans and the attention God lavished upon them. In his rebellion, he convinced legions of angels to follow him, leading to their downfall. God, in His infinite wisdom and mercy, had created both heaven and earth, and He loved His creations deeply. Lucifer's defiance corrupted his once-pure spirit, transforming him into a serpent who tempted humanity into committing the first sin. God's rule for all beings, celestial and human, is simple: to love one another as oneself. This rule, if followed, would ensure paradise for everyone. However, Lucifer's pride led him to deceive Eve, who then shared the forbidden fruit with Adam, bringing sin into the world.

Upon Lucifer's return to heaven, he found himself confronted by God's wrath. God, who had seen through Lucifer's deceit, cast him out of heaven with a force that shook the very foundations of the celestial realm. Heaven heard and felt God's anger as He chained Lucifer, marking him as the first to be judged by God's righteous hand.

God renamed Lucifer Satan and cast him into a place beneath the earth, a realm of eternal fire and suffering known as hell. This pit of lava would be Satan's dwelling, where he and all who followed him would suffer for eternity.

Eli reflects on this ancient tale, knowing that their current struggle is but a continuation of this age-old conflict. They are fighting not just for their lives but for the very soul of humanity. The lessons of the past—the fall of Lucifer and the enduring battle between good and evil—serve as a stark reminder of the stakes. With courage and faith, they move forward, ready to face whatever challenges lie ahead.

Before Lucifer takes his leave, he takes half of heaven's angels with him. They are all called the Fallen. Humans know them as demons. God descends to Earth to punish the husband and his wife for not obeying the only rule they needed to follow. Once naked, now covered because of the forbidden fruit, they see themselves very differently, as they truly are. God tells them both they are now to live outside the

Clash Between Hope and Despair

Garden of Paradise, to age, struggle, and perish of old age like the rest of His creations. They both ask for forgiveness, but it is too late. God has written it in the stars.

God explains to the first blessed that because of Lucifer's trickery, they will still have heaven's grace with His love and protection. Most importantly, God tells them that a demon who was once an angel, named Lucifer but now known as Satan, roams the earth with half of heaven's angels, who are now all demons. The Fallen, given dominion over Earth but cast out of heaven, will challenge humanity. God then commands them to have children, who will in turn have more children, to battle those who now hold dominion over the earth from hell. The earth belongs to the beings of light, the humans, created by the Celestial Gods.

The husband and his wife agree with God, turning away from the Garden but not away from their creator. They leave the Garden for the wilderness, determined to fulfill God's command. From that day on, the war between heaven, earth, and hell begins.

***

Down a dark road to an armory go two brave soldiers, a father and his son, searching for more weapons to protect themselves and fight for humanity. It seems like forever driving in the darkness. They grow impatient but keep their cool. Eli reassures his son that the armory is only three minutes away. After two and a half minutes, they see the armory once more.

As they pull into a large, gated parking lot, they see bodies draped over cars and gates, the remains of people who tried to climb over. Corpses are piled on top of each other, mostly military personnel who were supposed to be the mightiest in the world. Sadness overcomes Eli and his son, but they show no emotion. Eli tells his son to say a prayer for those who perished from the war on the cold dark concrete, by the hand of those from below.

Clash Between Hope and Despair

Eli and James step out of the truck, weapons ready. They carefully navigate through the sea of bodies, making their way to the armory entrance. The scene is somber, a grim reminder of the stakes of their mission. Despite the horrors around them, they focus on their task.

James finds a clear spot and kneels, bowing his head with respect. "May these souls find peace," he whispers, "and may their sacrifice not be in vain." Eli nods, gripping his rifle tighter, then gestures for James to follow him.

Inside, the armory is in disarray. Shelves overturned; crates shattered open. But there are still supplies—boxes of ammunition, rifles, and other weaponry scattered around. They quickly begin gathering what they need, prioritizing ammunition and any heavy artillery they can carry.

Suddenly, a noise from the shadows makes them freeze. Eli signals for silence, raising his rifle. They listen intently, hearing faint footsteps approaching. James positions himself behind a crate, ready to fire if necessary.

A figure emerges from the darkness—a young soldier, barely alive, dragging himself towards them.

"Help...please," he gasps, collapsing to the ground. Eli rushes over, checking his pulse. The soldier is alive but weak, clearly having endured much.

"James, get some water," Eli orders, and his son quickly complies. They give the soldier water, and he manages to speak, albeit faintly. "There are more...inside. We were attacked...demonites...they're still here."

Eli and James exchange determined looks. Their mission just became more urgent. They finish gathering supplies quickly and prepare to move deeper into the armory. They must save whoever they can and secure the weapons they need. The battle is far from over, and they must be ready for whatever comes next.

As Eli and his son enter the armory building, they make sure their weapons are locked and loaded, ready for any surprises.

***

Clash Between Hope and Despair

Back at the airport, Ethan and Charlie begin a new search for food and water inside the main facility.
They have been unsuccessful so far, finding only dried-out food and empty water pipes. Now on the third floor, they hear the echoes of water leaking from broken pipes. They carefully follow the sound, navigating past hanging wires and debris. Ethan warns Charlie to avoid the electrified water, and Charlie reassures him, staying alert as they approach the water source.
Charlie eagerly drinks from the leaking water pipe, quenching his thirst. Ethan goes into a nearby restaurant, searching for containers to carry the water back to the others. The restaurant is dark and smells of decay, filled with debris and the bodies of those killed by demon knights or the building's collapse. Ethan searches behind bars, on shelves, and in offices, finding everything broken or infested with maggots. Finally, he reaches the kitchen, hoping to find usable containers and food.
The kitchen is cool; there is still a functioning freezer.
Ethan finds three empty buckets and then searches the freezer for food. He finds vegetables wrapped in plastic, still fresh. He fills boxes with the vegetables and exits the first freezer, noticing chewed-up meat that suggests something has been feeding there. Ethan then enters the second freezer, hoping for more supplies.
Inside the second freezer, Ethan finds hanging frozen meat and decides to investigate further, despite the eerie feeling. As he pushes aside the hanging meat, he comes face to face with a massive beast, a hellhound from below, as big as a lion with the face of a dead dog, chewing on a piece of beef. Ethan ducks back into the hanging meat, but it is too late. The hellhound has heard him and is now sniffing him out. Ethan quickly loads his chamber, preparing for a battle with the monstrous creature. The hellhound's growl echoes in the frigid air, and Ethan knows he must act fast. He inches back toward the entrance of the freezer, trying to put distance

between him and the hellhound. The beast's eyes glow with a demonic fire as it stalks him through the hanging meat.

Ethan steadies his breath, knowing he has only one chance to take down the hellhound. He aims his rifle at the creature, waiting for the right moment. The hellhound pounces, and Ethan fires, the bullets tearing through the beast's flesh. The hellhound yelps in pain but keeps coming, driven by a relentless hunger. Ethan fires repeatedly, until the hellhound finally collapses, lifeless, onto the frozen floor.

Breathing heavily, Ethan lowers his rifle, his heart pounding. He quickly fills the buckets with water, grabs the boxes of vegetables, and rushes out of the freezer. He finds Charlie outside, still drinking from the pipe. "We need to go," Ethan says urgently. "Now."

Charlie looks up, sensing the urgency in Ethan's voice. He grabs a bucket and helps Ethan carry the supplies back to the others. They make their way back through the dark, debris-filled hallways, staying alert for any other dangers.

Meanwhile, at the armory, Eli and his son make their way through the building, finding the ammo and weapons they need. They load up their truck, ready to head back to the airport. As they drive back, Eli says a prayer for the fallen soldiers they saw, hoping their sacrifice will not be in vain.

At the airport, Adonis and Biggs continue working on the garbage trucks, making substantial progress. They hear Ethan and Charlie returning and see them carrying buckets of water and boxes of vegetables. Everyone gathers around, grateful for the supplies. They quickly distribute the water and food, replenishing their strength.

Eli and his son return shortly after, bringing much-needed ammo and weapons. The group is now better readied and more prepared for the battles ahead. They know the fight against the demon Knights, and hellhounds is far from over, but they are ready to face whatever comes next, determined to protect their humanity and their planet.

Ethan loads his rifle chamber and takes a deep breath, emerging from between the hanging meat to shoot the hellhound. But it is not there. Ethan cautiously moves to where the hellhound was gnawing on the frozen meat. Hearing a growl from behind, Ethan spins around just in time to see the hellhound lunging at him. The beast tackles him to the ground, causing Ethan to fire off rounds into the ceiling. Disarmed and on his stomach, Ethan manages to turn onto his back, grabbing the hellhound's jaws to prevent them from sinking into his flesh. The creature's hot breath and dripping saliva make it clear how close he is to death.

Just as Ethan's strength starts to wane, Charlie rushes in, having heard the gunshots. He unloads an entire magazine into the hellhound, forcing it off Ethan. The wounded beast retreats a couple steps, its body marked by deep claw gashes. Charlie extends a hand to help Ethan up, keeping his rifle trained on the hound.

"Are you alright?" Charlie asks, eyes still on the hellhound. "Yeah, thanks to you," Ethan replies, catching his breath. "I found some fresh vegetables in the freezer. We can take them back with the water."

Charlie grabs two buckets while Ethan takes the others. They do not notice the hellhound rapidly healing from its wounds. As they start to leave, the beast lets out a furious howl, signaling its intent to hunt them down. They drop the buckets, realizing they need to finish this fight. Both reload their rifles and turn back to face the beast.

The hellhound leaps onto a counter, eyes glowing red with rage. Saliva drips from its menacing teeth. "Oh shit," they mutter in unison, stepping back as the creature steps forward, ready to attack.

Ethan and Charlie sprint toward the stairs, but the hellhound is too fast, forcing them to take a detour through the building. The hound crashes into walls, its body indestructible. Ethan fires at it but misses, the bullets having no effect on the relentless beast.

Cornered at a dead end, they decide to fight. Behind them is a glass window overlooking the runway and in front is the hellhound, its hot breath visible as it prepares to strike.

Clash Between Hope and Despair

They load their rifles with special, classified ammunition, hoping it will be enough.

The hellhound charges, but Ethan and Charlie fire in unison, their bullets finding their mark. The beast roars in pain but keeps coming. It lunges at Charlie, knocking him to the ground and injuring his leg. Ethan jumps on the hound's back, wrapping his rifle around its throat. The hellhound, annoyed, shakes him off, throwing Ethan against the thick glass. The impact knocks Ethan unconscious, leaving him vulnerable.

The hellhound turns its attention back to Charlie. With a broken leg, Charlie crawls toward his rifle, but the hound crushes it under its massive paw. Charlie spits in the creature's face, showing defiance despite his situation. As the hound prepares to finish him, a series of loud shots ring out. Charlie hears the familiar sound of a heavy-caliber rifle.

The hellhound flies off its feet from the impact of the bullets. The shooting continues until the beast's chest stops heaving. Silence follows.

Charlie looked up, his vision blurred. He sees not God, but his cousin, Mike, and Josias standing with smoking M50 tank killers. Relief washes over him.

"You, okay?" Mike asks, helping Charlie to his feet.

"Just in time," Charlie responds, wincing in pain but grateful. The hellhound lies dead, its body finally still. They collect the vegetables and water, knowing their fight is not over but feeling a momentary victory.

Josias goes to Ethan while Mike goes to Charlie, helping him up. Charlie, still wary, warns Mike to watch the hellhound, explaining that it got back up after he shot it earlier. Mike reassures Charlie that the beast is dead, but Charlie, not taking any chances, grabs a machete from Mike's fatigue. He swings at the hellhound's neck, severing it after a sundry of strikes. He picks up the head and throws it into a nearby fire, ensuring it burns to ashes.

Josias helps Ethan to his feet, but Ethan, still dazed, falls back to his knees, asking for a moment to catch his breath.

Clash Between Hope and Despair

As Josias tries to assist him again, Charlie watches over the area.

Ethan, regaining his composure, walks beside Josias, and they all head back to the restaurant to gather the vegetables and water they found before the hellhound's attack.

They fill the buckets with water from the broken pipes. Ethan carries two water buckets, Mike and Josias each carry one, and Charlie, with his injured leg, ties a string from the box of vegetables to his waist, dragging it behind him as they exit the airport facility.

As they regroup and prepare to head back to the others, they know that together they stand a better chance against the horrors that roam their world. The war between heaven, earth, and hell is far from over, but they are ready to face whatever comes next.

***

Eli and James move cautiously toward the entrance to the armory, hoping to find the necessary supplies. They do not yet know that Babylon has left legions of his warriors behind, now guarding the armory. As they approach the familiar entrance they find it blocked with steel beams and cars, placed there intentionally.

Eli instructs James to find a way to move the debris. Realizing a garbage truck, they spotted earlier could do the job, they rush back to it. As they near the truck, three demon knights fly overhead, searching for intruders. Eli and James hide among the rotting corpses until the knights pass by, then proceed to the truck. Eli suggests putting the truck in neutral to avoid attracting attention. They move the truck slowly into the parking lot, with James pushing and Eli steering.

Once at the entrance, they attach chains from the truck to the steel beams. Eli reminds James that starting the truck will alert the demon knights. They agree to work quickly, hoping to fight inside the armory where there are more places to hide. With everything set, James jumps into the truck, ready to start the engine, while Eli stands guard with his modified M16.

As the engine roars to life, the truck pulls the debris away from the entrance with a deafening crash. The noise echoes throughout the armory, drawing the attention of the demon knights. Eli and James take cover as the demon knights investigate the noise.

Inside, the demon knights find nothing but empty crates and the cleared entrance. Eli and James, hiding behind the crates, prepare for a fight. They need to secure the extra artillery for their next battle with Babylon. Adrenalines coursing through their veins, they silently ready their weapons, determined to overcome whatever stands in their way.

As the demon knights search the ground floor, Eli and James know a confrontation is imminent. They brace themselves, hoping to turn the tide in their favor and secure the armory's weapons to aid their allies in the war against the dragon Babylon and his hellish forces.

As the demon knights enter the armory their eyes glow bright red, yellow, and orange, enhancing their sight in the darkness. They search for the intruders, unaware that Eli and his son James are hiding among the crates above them.

Eli signals James to crawl toward the rear wall to set up an ambush. One demon knight releases yellow beams from his mouth, igniting the crates in an attempt to expose anyone hiding.

The fire spreads quickly, and the two humans know they must act fast before the building is devoured by the flames. The demon knights separate to cover more ground, giving Eli and James the opportunity to pick them off one by one. The demon with the orange eyes moves between the crates, sniffing for intruders. Eli and James follow, waiting for the right moment.

As the demon knight stops to sniff again, Eli and James leap from behind the crates and unload their clips into its chest. The demon's eyes and mouth flare with light, brighter than the sun, before it collapses, blowing out a wall and throwing

Clash Between Hope and Despair

James into another pile of crates. Though not knocked out, James suffers a gash on his forehead, blood blinding him. Eli lifts his son, wiping the blood from his eyes and applying pressure to the wound.

James recovers enough to wrap his forehead with a piece of cloth from his fatigues, urging his father to hurry before the fire reaches the ammunition. They move to the next floor, the darkness growing denser. Their eyes adjust to the red glow as they ascend the stairs. Unbeknownst to them a demon knight hovers above, watching their every move, waiting for its companion to join the hunt.

Eli and James split up, prioritizing the elimination of the remaining demon knights over finding the weapons. The second floor is an open, empty space, perfect for a confrontation. Accuracy will be crucial in the dark, open environment. Through a broken window, the third demon knight, previously patrolling outside, enters the building.

Eli and James take their positions, ready for the fight. The hovering demon knight descends silently, its glowing eyes searching for the humans. Eli, hidden behind a pillar, takes aim at the approaching demon. With precision, he fires, hitting the demon knight in its chest. It screeches, its eyes flaring a bright red, but it does not fall.

James, hearing the screech, fires at the demon knight from another angle, his bullets hitting home. The demon thrashes but remains standing. Knowing they need to finish it off, Eli and James converge, firing in unison. The demon knight finally collapses, its body hitting the floor with a heavy thud. As they catch their breath, the last demon knight, seeing its fallen comrade, rushes toward them. Eli and James prepare for the final showdown, their hearts pounding. They know this is their last chance to secure the weapons and return to their family.

The final demon knight charges, its eyes glowing fiercely. Eli and James, standing side by side, fire at the advancing creature. Bullets rip through the air, hitting the demon. It stumbles but keeps coming, its determination fueled by rage. Eli and James press on, their magazines nearly empty.

In a desperate move the demon knight leaps at them, but Eli grabs a nearby metal rod and swings with all his might. The rod connects with the demon's head, sending it crashing to the ground. James quickly unloads his last bullets into the demon knight, ensuring it does not get back up.

Breathing heavily, Eli and James look at each other, relieved but aware that the fire is spreading. They need to find the weapons quickly. They rush to the storage area, now clear of the demon knights. Among the crates, they find much-needed ammunition and weapons.

With their new arsenal in hand, they hurry to the next floor, navigating through the growing flames. As they run they hear the sound of wind. They know that the rushing sound they hear is from the wings of the demon knights, as there has been no natural wind since the chaos began. In a panic, the two split up, taking different paths to the second floor.

James, aware that demons are pursuing them, is filled with paranoia about his father's safety. Both father and son head for the second floor, trying to reunite.

On the second floor, James spots the glowing eyes of the two demon knights. He points his modified M-16 at them just as one of the demon knight's eyes begin to glow intensely.

This demon is preparing to unleash a powerful attack. The other demon knight exhales a stream of glowing smoke that forms fireballs which hit the floor in front of James, causing the ground to collapse beneath him. James falls through to the sub-basement, landing on a pile of crates and knocking himself out.

Eli, on the opposite side of the second floor, sees his son fall and charges toward the spot, firing his M-16 at the demon knights. The demons retaliate with their mystical powers. One of them uses telekinesis to fling Eli across the floor, knocking his weapon from his hands and leaving him vulnerable.

Clash Between Hope and Despair

Fueled by rage and grief, believing his son might be dead, Eli fights with newfound ferocity. He dodges the demon knights' attacks with agility, finally landing a shot that brings one demon down temporarily. However, Eli runs out of ammo, and he is involuntarily forced to his knees by a telekinetic blow from the remaining airborne demon knight.

Despite being weaponless and weakened, Eli channels his pain into strength. The grounded demon charges at him, but Eli uses his martial arts skills to flip the demon knight out of a window, impaling it on a garbage truck below. The demon's death scream echoes through the area, alerting the others and awakening James in the sub-basement.

James, now conscious, finds himself on top of a box filled with weapons. He grabs a rocket launcher and some rockets and makes his way back to the second floor. Meanwhile, Eli continues to fight the remaining demon knight with his bare hands. As the demon prepares to snap Eli's neck, Eli manages to free himself and drops to the floor.

James reaches the second floor and signals for his father to duck. Eli, understanding the signal, uses his remaining strength to knock the demon knight's hands away and drops to the floor. James fires the rocket, which hits the demon square in the chest, propelling it through the wall and outside, where it explodes into pieces.

James rushes to his father's side. Eli, after falling, has been tolerably injured and dazed, his body covered in blood. James helps Eli up, reassuring him they have won this battle.

They know that the fight against Babylon and his minions is far from over, but for now they have each other and the weapons they need to protect their family.

James lifts his father, Eli, to his feet and informs him of the substantial cache of weapons and ammo he found in the sub-basement. Eli, catching his breath, realizes the urgency of their situation as the fire continues to spread from the ground floor. If they do not get out soon, the entire building will explode from the ammunition below.

Clash Between Hope and Despair

Eli nods in agreement. "We need to move fast," he says, his voice steady despite his injuries. "We can't afford to lose these weapons. They could turn the tide for everyone back in New York City."

James, determined, replies, "Let's gather as much as we can carry. We can drop the weapons from the sky to supply the people on the ground while we focus on airstrikes to eliminate Babylon."

Both father and son rush down to the sub-basement to gather the arsenal they need to battle the demons from hell. Once there, they realize the only way to take the weapons outside is to go back up the stairs and back down, which is impossible, because the building is still burning to the ground. They both pause, frustrated and thinking of a way to get the weapons out, but taking too long will get them burned alive.

The intensity of the situation frustrates James, who kicks over crates of weapons, revealing a small window hidden behind the crates. Eli calls him a genius and rushes to the window, breaking the glass, since it does not open. They quickly notice the window is too small to fit the needed crates, but without hesitation they grab a crate each, shoving them through the broken window as fast as they can to avoid further delays or being incinerated alive. They take the smallest crates first, clearing them out within a minute and leaving about thirteen big crates.

Exhausted but determined, they immediately go to the bigger crates, hoping they can fit through the window.

Carrying one big crate together at a time, they realize there is no way the crate could ever fit through the small window. Eli suggests trying to turn the crate while pushing it through the window, but it still does not work. Frustrated, they try one more time, forcing the crate through, and, miraculously, the window stretches itself as if helping them push the crate through. They do not notice what happened and think their method worked, unaware of the mystical forces assisting them.

Clash Between Hope and Despair

Within moments the room is cleared, except for two crates they cannot get due to the deadly smoke and fire. But leaving two crates is better than leaving their lives behind. With the burning building behind them, they load the garbage trucks with all the crates they can, putting the rest on top and securing them with chains used to pull the steel beams from the entrance.

As they get into the garbage trucks, the roof of the building explodes from the gas pipes still active inside. Eli slams on the gas pedal, the dead demon knight still hanging from the exhaust pipe, running over dead bodies and breaking through the gate, taking a different route instead of the way they came. Finally, they are on the street, speeding toward the airport.

As they speed down the dark road, the flames from the burning building are the only thing visible in the distance. Eli and James thank God for protecting them during the crisis. They hear the facility explode again, as if hit by a missile by stealth fighters or mech fighters. James wonders what could have caused such a furious explosion, thanking God for getting them out alive. Eli frowns, telling his son the two crates of C4 and dynamite left behind could have been useful in the fight for New York City. James asks how he knew it was explosive, and Eli replies that the crates had "EXPLOSIVES" written in big red letters. Eli adds, "Why do you think I rushed us out of there so fast?"

***

The explosion of the armory is heard back at the airport. It is so dark the explosion can be observed by all who heard it, and the sound is unmistakable. Everyone's attention is drawn to the explosion, hoping Eli and James made it out alive. Biggs and his brother Josias run to the middle of the road outside the airport, staring into the darkness, the dense light from the fire blazing in the distance. Josias tells Biggs not to think negatively, reminding him that their father, Eli, always finds a way out of any situation, even those from hell. They agree to give Eli and James ten minutes to return; if not, they will go to the explosion site to ensure any remaining demons are destroyed.

The rest of the team stands behind Biggs and Josias, feeling the same determination and readiness to confront any challenge to humanity's existence. Shoulder to shoulder, they wait, ready to act if their companions do not return.

Josias clenches his right fist so tightly that blood starts to drip from his knuckles. He stares at his bleeding hand and tells Mike to get the garbage truck ready, preparing for the possibility that they may need to go on a rescue mission or take further action against any surviving demons.

As Mike steps forward, his brother, Gage, calls out to delay the request, pointing out that a vehicle is already approaching. Josias looks up from his bleeding hand with a look of relief and mutters a prayer, asking his god for forgiveness for doubting their deliverance. The group remains where they are, prepared to assist if Eli and James need help. The lights from the approaching garbage truck grow brighter, revealing boxes on its roof and what looks like a dead body hanging from the exhaust pipe. The truck pulls up, and they recognize the body as a deceased demon knight. Eli stops the truck, and his sons open the doors to help him and James out, eager to learn what happened at the armory and how the demon ended up on the truck. Josias takes the driver's seat as the others help Eli and James back to the airport. As Josias drives off, Biggs shares good news with his father: they have found water and vegetables, a welcome relief after their ordeal. Eli and James are grateful for the chance to quench their thirst after narrowly escaping the smoky inferno.

The night is calm as the group reunites. The only sounds are the truck's engine and the rustling of plastic covering the bodies of those killed by hell's forces. The sight and smell are heart-wrenching, but they find solace in burying their fallen comrades and blessing the soil, wishing they could bring them back to life.

Hours pass as they complete the burials, exhausted from the night's events. With little rest, they prepare to head back to New York City, determined to free those still suffering under the claws of the Great Dragon Babylon. This time they bring with them not just weapons, but a renewed sense of hope and determination to fight back against the forces of hell.

After the burial for the fallen concludes, everyone focuses on the arsenal of weapons brought back from the military armory. They carefully sort and match each weapon with its corresponding ammunition, organizing them into crates. Once the weapons are primed and ready for action, Mike secures the crates to the bottom of the mech fighters and stealth fighters, ensuring they can be detached mid-flight over New York City.

Charlie, observing the preparations, asks Eli if he really believes the people, tormented under the Great Dragon Babylon's rule, will rise and use these weapons. Eli replies confidently, explaining that if he were in their shoes, he would see these weapons as a divine gift. Charlie concedes that while Eli is a natural warrior, all these people have spent months in fear. Despite this, Eli insists it is worth trying to inspire them to fight back.

The next crucial task is to find fuel for the mechs and gather more ammunition, especially missiles. Josias approaches Eli, asking where they can find jet fuel at the airport, given the damage inflicted by the demons. Eli suggests checking the sub-basement, where various fuel lines are still intact. He mentions there should be the jet fuel they need.

They form two teams to reconnaissance the sub-basement. As they descend, they realize they will need to endure an extensive network of pipes. Encouraged by the fact that the electricity is still operational, indicating a separate power source, they focus on finding the jet fuel. Eli's team, consisting of his three sons and their friend Ethan, finally locates pipes for regular and diesel fuel, but not jet fuel. Disheartened, they started to head back.

On their way back, Ethan notices a faintly glowing rectangular outline in a wall. He calls the others over and they decide to investigate. Josias quickly finds an override switch, revealing a hidden control room. Meanwhile, Mike's team, consisting of his brother and cousins, along with their friend Adonis, continues their search. They too are close to discovering something significant.

In the control room, Eli's team finds a wealth of information. The room, unknown to all, holds controls and schematics for the entire airport's fuel system. This hidden room might be their key to accessing jet fuel. As they scan the controls, they realize they can override the system to direct jet fuel to a specific location.

Simultaneously, Mike's team reaches the end of their search. Mike decides to investigate a mysterious pipeline alone, which is the jet fuel line they have been looking for.

As he follows the line, he confirms it leads to a fuel depot specifically for jets.

With both teams close to their goals, they communicate their findings. Eli's team prepares to redirect the jet fuel, while Mike's team sets up the necessary equipment to pump the fuel to the surface. They coordinate their efforts, ensuring they can refuel the mech fighters and stealth fighters efficiently.

In the control room, Eli's team manages to activate the fuel pumps, directing the jet fuel to a central location. Mike and his team are ready with hoses and pumps, quickly transferring the fuel to the mechs. The operation progresses smoothly, and everyone feels a surge of hope. They now have the fuel needed to return to New York City and provide the people with the means to fight back against their oppressors.

Back at the hidden control room, Eli's team continues to explore. They find various computers analyzing activities across the United States and revealing more secret bases around the country, except one back in New York City. Biggs discovers shelves filled with the airport's engineering plans, including certain files labeled for military personnel only. Among these plans, he finds a diagram indicating that the outer field of the airport is a missile launch area, prepared for wartime scenarios.

Biggs shares this information with the others, who are still searching for clues about who was running this command room. However, typical of the military, there is no identifiable information. Josias then discovers another hidden room near their location. It leads to a deeper area, which turns out to be a warehouse for the missiles located in the fields of North Carolina airport. Realizing the potential of this discovery, Eli sends his two sons back to Mike to fetch Charlie and Hunter, hoping they can figure out how to operate the system they've found.

Biggs and Josias quickly head back to the meeting point where Mike and the rest of the team are already waiting, ready to refuel the fighters and return to New York City. When Mike sees only the two brothers approaching, he immediately fears the worst, asking if something happened to the rest of the team or their father, Eli. Josias reassures him, explaining that everyone is fine. He then tells Mike about their incredible findings and emphasizes the need for Charlie and Hunter's expertise.

Mike takes a deep breath, telling both brothers to lead the way to the others. Despite feeling they might be wasting time, everyone follows, driven by curiosity and the hope of gaining an advantage. They walk for a couple of minutes before arriving at the hidden room within the airport. With the door closed, Mike asks Biggs where the place is. Biggs turns to the concrete wall and activates an override switch, revealing the hidden missile launch command center. Everyone's eyes widen in surprise.

Charlie tells Hunter it should be remarkably interesting, especially if they find something dependable. They all step inside, finding Eli's team already trying to get the system back online and uncovering valuable information about the missiles.

Charlie and Hunter start working on separate computers, their fingers moving rapidly. Charlie discovers a recorded message from one of the personnel who was there before being dispatched by a demon horde. He calls everyone's attention to the big screen. The screen turns blue, showing a picture of an individual who explains the current situation and what the system is capable of if used correctly. The person mentions it is part of the advanced Star Wars project, with about eight satellites orbiting Earth, ready to go online and awaiting commands. He explains the functionality of the system and gives code words to bring it online: Delta, Gamma, Alpha, Luke, and Oblivion. In the background, screams, gunfire, and demonic roars are heard, causing visible shivers. The man picks up an M16, wishes himself good luck, and the video ends with the sound of gunfire and screams.

Realizing the potential of the system, Mike tells Charlie and Hunter to bring it online. Eli asks Mike to show him where the jet fuel is so they can prepare the fighters. Ethan, Adonis, Biggs, Gage, Eli, and Josias accompany Mike, while Charlie and Hunter stay behind to figure out how to operate the satellite system.

They quickly reach the jet fuel tanks and find a way to pump the fuel to the surface for the fighters. They go to the surface, refueling all the fighters and ensuring the crates of weapons are intact, ready to be dropped in New York City.

Josias returns alone to inform Hunter and Charlie they are about to leave. He gives them the frequency to stay in contact and salutes them before leaving. Charlie promises a surprise when they return.

As Josias emerges, he sees the entire airport lit up, with everyone inside their stealth fighter mechs and ready for takeoff. He smiles briefly before returning to a battle-ready expression. He salutes his companions as they prepare for takeoff, the air compressors hissing. Josias knows they are ready for anything hell throws at them.

Clash Between Hope and Despair

The fighters take off, leaving the airport behind. Josias proceeds to his fighter, feeling a mix of anticipation and determination. He knows they have a crucial mission ahead, and with the missile system potentially providing an edge they might just turn the tide in their favor.

With everyone united and prepared, they head toward New York City, ready to face the forces of hell and reclaim humanity's future.

The fighters, now tiny specks in the sky, continue their journey as Josias closes his cockpit and starts his engines to full throttle. He contacts Charlie, instructing him to turn off the lights in sixty seconds to avoid attracting unwanted attention. Charlie responds with a "Roger that," and Josias lifts off, racing to catch up with the others.

***

Meanwhile, in New York City, the dragon Babylon is feasting when he suddenly senses a disturbance. He feels tense, knowing the flying machines are returning to challenge him. He informs Berserker, who is standing by his side, to prepare for battle. Babylon gathers more demon knights and others to take to the skies, hoping to spot the machines before they arrive.

Although Berserker is disturbed by Babylon's lack of trust in his instincts, he remains silent to avoid incurring Babylon's wrath.

The imprisoned people below notice Babylon's agitation, hoping it signifies the arrival of their saviors.

***

Back at the North Carolina airport, Charlie and Hunter finally get the system online. The main screen shows a clear satellite view of the airport and its surroundings. They evaluate the system by pinpointing a small object in Florida with incredible precision. Ecstatic, they realize they can now control the satellite's lasers, missiles, and other armaments. They direct the satellites' views toward New York City and keep one overhead for additional support.

Renaming the system "Oblivion," they understand there is more to learn, but they already have the crucial functionality in hand. They zoom in on New York City, enhancing the view to see the people trapped by the dragon Babylon and other demon knights. One camera gets a close-up of Babylon's multiple heads, though the brothers do not yet realize an arch demon is also present.

Charlie and Hunter notify Eli and Mike about their progress. Mike advises them to hold off on any action until they arrive in New York City, planning to surprise their enemies with unexpected firepower.

The brothers then focus on finding the best drop points for the weapons, observing the people hiding in abandoned or destroyed buildings. Charlie is bursting with anger at the sight, eager to unleash the satellites' power on the demons. Hunter advises caution, reminding Charlie not to reveal their capabilities prematurely. He contacts the mech fighters, updating them on their position over Virginia and estimating their arrival in New York City in about ten minutes.

Remembering Josias's mention of another hidden room in the airport, Charlie and Hunter search for the engineering plans. They find the relevant plan, ensuring everything is calm and operational before heading to explore the hidden room.

Back in New York City, the tension mounts as Babylon and his forces prepare for the impending confrontation. The enslaved people sense a glimmer of hope, knowing their rescuers are drawing near. Meanwhile, the fighters speed toward the city, determined to reclaim it from the clutches of hell.

In the hidden room, Charlie and Hunter find advanced control systems and weaponry, realizing they have more at their disposal than they initially thought. They plan to use these resources strategically to support the fighters and the people on the ground.

Clash Between Hope and Despair

As the fighters near New York City, the brothers finalize their preparations, ready to coordinate the attack with pinpoint accuracy. The stage is set for a battle that will determine the fate of humanity, with the advanced technology of the Oblivion System providing a crucial edge in their fight against the forces of hell.

Charlie and Hunter give themselves ten minutes to explore the hidden warehouse before returning to the Oblivion System Control Center. Upon reaching the secret room, they find it concealed behind two soda machines.

Following the sequence of button presses indicated in the plans, the machines release a cloud of smoke and hiss as they slide apart, revealing a door to a previously unknown room. Stepping inside, they find the room dark and eerie. Charlie, recalling the location of the switches from the floor plans, navigates the darkness and flips them on, illuminating a massive warehouse stocked with an array of weapons, advanced mech tanks, and other resources. Overwhelmed with excitement, the brother's high five each other and take a quick tour, discovering a section filled with specialized ammo for the jet fighters—ammunition they wish they had had earlier.

After a brief look around, they rush back to the missile control room, leaving the warehouse doors open for a quick return. They hear Josias over the receiver, who has just started trying to contact them. Hunter responds, and Josias informs them they are over New Jersey and will reach New York City in about two minutes. The brothers quickly take their positions, ready to be the eyes in the sky for the fighters. Josias informs the rest of the fighters that everything is in place and they are moments away from engaging in battle. Charlie opens communication lines to each mech fighter to share the news about the hidden warehouse.

He starts by saying it is not just another room but something exciting. Mike, impatient, urges him to get to the point. Charlie reveals the warehouse abounds with an advanced arsenal of weapons and materials, including extra ammo they can ship back to New York City to help the people reclaim their humanity. Eli acknowledges the good news, but Charlie continues, detailing the additional arsenal of missiles, mechs for the stealth fighters, and even a fully loaded mech tank they can use against the hell demons on the ground.

The fighters listen intently as Charlie emphasizes the significance of this discovery, ensuring them they have the firepower to make a significant impact in their battle against the demonic forces. With the Oblivion System online and the warehouse's resources at their disposal, they feel more confident about their chances.

As they approach New York City, the atmosphere is tense but filled with a sense of purpose. The enslaved people below sense that their saviors are near, and the fighters, equipped with newfound hope and advanced technology, prepare to engage in what they hope will be the final confrontation to reclaim their city and humanity's future.

Josias and his team prepare to drop the weapon crates for the people on the ground, coordinating with Charlie and Hunter for precise targeting. The stage is set for an epic showdown, with the advanced arsenal and the strategic advantage of the Oblivion System giving the fighters a fighting chance against Babylon and his demonic army.

The fighters, knowing the stakes, are resolute in their mission. They believe that fighting and dying is far preferable to living under the torment of hell's demon army. Upon reaching their destination, they are greeted by a formidable barricade of demon knights, standing as the last line of defense between the enslaved people and the hope of salvation. With precision, each of the eight stealth fighters target specific points along the demon knight line, ensuring that their limited firepower is used precisely and effectively. They unleash a volley of explosive miniature missiles, with each fighter firing two, strategically hitting the middle, right, and left ends of the barricade. The explosion tears through the demon line, creating a path straight to the dragon Babylon and the designated drop point for the weapon crates.

Clash Between Hope and Despair

Unbeknownst to the fighters, the arch demon Berserker, a legendary warrior feared throughout hell, stands ready to engage them. As Berserker prepares to take to the skies, Babylon instructs him to hold back. Babylon wants the demon knights already in the air to deplete the fighters' resources first, making it easier for Berserker to deal with them later. Frustrated but obedient, Berserker questions this strategy, craving the glory of battle.

Babylon, in a display of authority, turns one of his massive heads toward Berserker, smoke billowing from his nostrils as a warning. He asks if Berserker is challenging his command. Berserker, though seething with anger, knows better than to defy Babylon openly. He bows his head, acknowledging Babylon's authority, and reassures him that he would never disobey an order from his superior.

With the barricade broken, the stealth fighters quickly deploy the crates of weapons, releasing them to the people below. The civilians, hiding in the ruins of New York City, watch with a mix of hope and trepidation as the supplies parachute down. They know this is their chance to fight back against the demonic oppression.

As the crates land, the fighters above keep a vigilant eye on the demon knights and their movements. Babylon, still watching from his vantage point, senses the impending conflict and prepares his forces. The demon knights in the sky begin to converge on the stealth fighters, engaging in an aerial battle that will assess the pilots' skills and resolve.

Charlie and Hunter, from the Oblivion System Control Center, monitor the situation closely. They see the unfolding battle through the satellites, pinpointing enemy positions and relaying crucial information to the fighters.

The brothers understand the critical role they play in this fight and are ready to unleash the full power of the Oblivion System when the time comes.

On the ground, the civilians scramble to open the crates, arming themselves with the weapons inside. Determined to reclaim their city and freedom, they prepare to join the fight, knowing the survival of humanity depends on their courage and unity.

The stage is set for an epic confrontation. The fighters in the sky, the civilians on the ground, and the brothers in the control center are all united in their determination to defeat the forces of hell. The battle for New York City and the future of humanity is about to begin, and each person knows that their actions in the coming moments will determine the outcome of this desperate struggle.

The eight stealth fighters push through the chaotic swarm of falling demon knights from the weakened barricade ordered by Babylon. Despite encountering more demons, the pilots maintain their resolve, undeterred by the increasing numbers. Eli, the father figure and leader, urges his companions to make every shot count, emphasizing their primary goal: to drop the weapon crates and then focus on annihilating Babylon, along with his seven grotesque heads. Their mission is clear: to inspire hope in the beleaguered civilians by crushing hell's army.

With precision and determination, the pilots launch their mini missiles, accurately targeting and eliminating the oncoming demon knights. The fighters then split into pairs to divert the demons, who prefer to hunt in packs like wolves. Each pair executes intricate maneuvers, leading groups of demon knights away from the civilians to clear the drop points. Adonis and Ethan head toward the Bronx, hoping to find an area devoid of civilians and tall buildings that might obstruct their battle. Mike and his brother Gage navigate toward upper Manhattan, instinctively choosing the Harlem area. Eli, accompanied by his son James, roams the entire city, assisting other pairs and drawing demon knights away from the ground. Biggs and Josias hover near Babylon, eager to strike first and armed with an abundance of rifles and ammunition.

Their actions are not just tactical but symbolic. It is time for humanity to reclaim their spirit and fight back against the forces of hell. As Biggs and Josias fly over a crowd of desperate civilians, they release the weapon crates, which shatter upon landing, scattering weapons for the people to seize. The brothers then engage the demon knights with unerring accuracy, clearing a path toward Babylon.

As the civilians below scramble to arm themselves, their despair transforms into a spark of hope. The sight of their fellow humans fighting back against the demonic onslaught ignites a newfound determination. People begin to gather weapons, ready to join the battle for their freedom.

Biggs and Josias, their hearts filled with a righteous fury, turn their attention to the dragon Babylon. With calculated precision, they fire at the monstrous beast, aiming to eliminate the current leader of Hell's invasion. Babylon, sensing the imminent threat, unleashes a deafening roar, shaking the very foundations of the city. His seven heads move with terrifying synchronicity, ready to confront the human challenge.

In the control center, Charlie and Hunter monitor the battle, providing real-time updates and guidance to the fighters. The Oblivion System's advanced technology allows them to target critical points with unparalleled accuracy. They prepare to unleash the full power of the system, coordinating with the fighters for a decisive strike.

AXIOM: OF THE
INDOMITABLE HUMAN SPIRIT
AXIOM

CHAPTER FOUR.
ARRIVAL
OF HOPE

Arrival of Hope

The battle over New York City rages on, a fierce testament to human resilience and defiance. The fighters, both in the sky and on the ground, unite with a single purpose: to reclaim their world from the clutches of hell. The air is filled with the sounds of conflict, but also with the unyielding spirit of those who refuse to surrender.

As the civilians join the fight, the tide begins to turn. The demon knights, a vast, fierce legion, collide with a wall of human resistance. The weapons from the crates give the civilians a fighting chance, and their collective effort begins to push back the demonic horde.

Babylon, now fully aware of the coordinated assault, finds himself facing not just the pilots but an entire city rising against him. His arrogance and sense of invincibility waver as the humans, bolstered by their newfound hope and determination, fight with a ferocity he had underestimated. The stage is set for a final, epic confrontation. The fate of New York City, and the entire world, hangs in the balance. Humanity stands at the brink of either reclamation or obliteration, ready to face whatever hell throws at them with unwavering courage.

Biggs and Josias, knowing they cannot defeat the dragon Babylon alone, turn their stealth fighters away to engage more demon knights. Biggs radios Eli, informing him that the weapon crates have been successfully dropped at the designated area. Eli, along with James, prepares for the second drop, while Biggs and Josias focus on keeping the demon knights at bay, ensuring the path remains clear.

Eli acknowledges the message, instructing his sons to hold the line for another minute until they arrive. Biggs and Josias comply, executing evasive maneuvers and engaging the demons to divert their attention. Their efforts are relentless, ensuring no demon interferes with the critical supply drop. Within sixty seconds, Eli and James soar behind the brothers, vigorously pursued by over a dozen demon knights.

Arrival of Hope

These creatures unleash hellish attacks in the form of miniature fireballs, molten flames, and searing beams of fire—but Biggs and Josias's skillful flying attracts the demon knights' aggression, giving Eli and James the opening they need. They maneuver through the chaos, deploying more weapon crates to the civilians below.

The people, initially paralyzed by fear, watch as the crates scatter on the ground. Eli radios Ethan, ordering him to return to downtown Manhattan to drop his load and join the fight. Ethan, engaged in a fierce battle, responds with urgency. He calls Adonis, instructing him to head back toward Babylon. Adonis, after downing dozens of demon knights, activates his hypersonic speed, vanishing in an instant.

Surrounded by demon knights, Ethan executes sharp turns and evasive maneuvers, creating an opening to escape. As he accelerates a demon clings to the rear of his fighter, tearing pieces off the craft. Ethan's afterburners incinerate the demon knight, but the damage to his stealth fighter is severe. He remains unaware that his craft might not make it back to North Carolina.

Adonis and Ethan reach the drop point with explosive precision, cutting through a cluster of demon knights. They release their weapon crates and swiftly turn to join their companions. Adonis radios Mike, urging him to hurry with his drop. Mike assures him that he and Gage are on their way, having faced minimal resistance. Gage takes over the receiver, informing Adonis they are just seconds behind.

Adonis shifts to the right, allowing Mike and Gage to zoom past. They fire upon Babylon, striking his chest and dropping the weapon crates before turning back to engage the dragon. Their electromagnetic weapons, lasers, and mini missiles find their mark, hitting Babylon's legs and upper torso. The dragon staggers, momentarily vulnerable.

Mike rallies the fighters, ordering them to concentrate all the firepower on Babylon. The stealth fighters, momentarily ignoring the demon knights, unleash their remaining ammunition at the dragon. Explosions surround Babylon, who roars in pain and fury. Berserker, caught in the crossfire, waits for Babylon's command to retaliate.

The relentless assault begins to change the tide of the battle. Babylon's temporary vulnerability offers the civilians a glimmer of hope. As the dragon thrashes, the demon knights falter, witnessing their leader's struggle. The fighters continue their barrage, aiming for the dragon's heads, determined to show the demon army their mighty leader can be defeated.

With renewed vigor, the people on the ground, inspired by the fighters' bravery, start picking up the scattered weapons. They prepare to join the battle, no longer content to remain helpless. This moment marks the beginning of humanity's fight for survival and reclamation of their world.

The battle intensifies as the fighters converge on Babylon, each strike bringing them closer to their goal. The dragon's roars echo through the city, the desperate sound of a beast realizing it may not be invincible. The fighters' coordinated efforts, combined with the civilians' newfound courage, create a formidable force against the hellish invaders.

The fate of New York City, and potentially the entire world, hinges on this confrontation. Humanity stands united, ready to reclaim their freedom and restore hope.

As the final showdown with Babylon unfolds, the determination and resilience of those fighting ensure that the struggle for their future is far from over.

Babylon, dripping with thick orange blood, realizes the severity of the threat posed by the stealth fighters. One of his heads hangs lifeless, a casualty of the humans' assault. Screaming in fury, Babylon commands the arch demon knight Berserker to avenge him. The fighters, knowing they have dealt damage but not enough to destroy Babylon, realize their ammo is depleted. Only Josias's fighter has any rounds left, but he is advised to retreat with the others.

On the ground, fires and thick smoke obscure the battlefield. The stealth fighters dodge and weave through the sky, awaiting the right moment to escape. Suddenly, a mighty

Arrival of Hope

demon knight with a double-edged axe emerges from the smoke—Berserker, his eyes glowing like suns, charges at them.

The sky clears as the demon knights make way for Berserker. The fighters break for North Carolina, but Berserker is close behind Ethan's plane, with Josias just ahead. Ethan breaks off, hoping to draw Berserker away. In a desperate maneuver, Ethan tries to eject but finds the button jammed.

Just as Berserker is about to strike, Josias arrives, firing his remaining rounds and knocking Berserker's axe from his hands. Josias tells Ethan to escape, assuring him he will handle Berserker. Ethan speeds away, disappearing into the night.

Josias, alone and low on ammo, faces Berserker. He maneuvers skillfully, avoiding Berserker's hellfire spheres, and fires a barrage of armor-piercing bullets, hitting Berserker's legs. Josias leads Berserker toward the Atlantic Ocean to avoid endangering those below.

Amid the battle, Josias contacts Biggs, informing him of the delay. Biggs, relieved to hear from his brother, urges him to return safely. Josias prepares for a final showdown, knowing he must make his last shots count. Berserker launches a series of attacks, but Josias dodges skillfully, responding with a final barrage that hits Berserker in the chest.

Berserker, enraged, threatens the people below, but Josias emerges from the clouds, unleashing his last rounds on Berserker. The demon knight is momentarily stunned, but as Josias flies through the smoke Berserker tears off the bottom of his stealth fighter. Josias shakes Berserker loose and attempts hypersonic speed, but the damaged fighter fails to respond.

As Josias struggles to control the falling plane, Berserker delivers a fatal blow, splitting the mech in two. Josias tries to eject, but the mechanism is destroyed. In a final act of defiance, Josias blows up the cockpit glass and fires at Berserker, declaring his determination to return and seek

Arrival of Hope

vengeance. Berserker, glowing with hellfire, unleashes a furious attack, obliterating the cockpit.

***

Back at the North Carolina airport, Hunter and Charlie restore power to the facility, unaware of Josias's fate. The battle rages on, the Hope of humanity, perilous.

Josias's sacrifice inspires those left behind, fueling their resolve to continue the fight against the forces of hell. The struggle is far from over, but the spirit of those who resist remains unbroken.

All cameras operational, all receivers active, Biggs urgently attempts to contact his brother. Responding swiftly, they hear Biggs instructing them to locate Josias in New York City and ensure his safe return to North Carolina. But as they manipulate the satellite cameras, horror and grief wash over them as they witness Josias's mech fighter crashing into the Atlantic Ocean. Tears of anger and vengeance fill their eyes as they watch the remnants of their brother's fighter sink beneath the waves.

"Oh my God," escapes their lips in unison. They turn the Oblivion System toward Berserker, focusing the arch demon knight in their crosshairs. They power up the system, targeting all eight Oblivion satellites at Berserker. Before firing, they exchange a solemn glance, whispering, "This one's for Josias." The satellites fire, each shot striking Berserker and hurling him into Babylon. Berserker falls to the ground, motionless.

Babylon, stunned, questions if he has been struck by divine intervention or something beyond the comprehension of mere mortals. Hunter volunteers to deliver the heart-wrenching news to Josias's family, a message he dreads conveying. Opening all lines to the remaining fighters, Hunter announces Josias's victory over hell's army and honors him as a warrior angel. Silence follows the announcement, a heavy, grief-laden silence.

Arrival of Hope

Suddenly, a heart-wrenching scream fills the radio— Biggs's scream of loss and pain. Nearly losing control of his fighter, Biggs is calmed by Eli's voice, who reassures him that Josias's soul is now at peace in God's arms.

Charlie switches on the airport lights, guiding the seven remaining stealth fighters to a safe landing. They disembark, their hearts heavy with the loss of Josias, their resolve steeled to continue the fight.

Entering the missile command center, they arm themselves, intent on incinerating the cursed ground the demons occupy. As they step into the airport's sub-basement, the outside lights shut off, engulfing the area in darkness. Their movements slow, they hear each other's heartbeats, unified in their determination to exact vengeance on hell.

Hunter and Charlie, anticipating their needs, lead them to a hidden location within the airport. The room, revealed to the seven fighters for the first time, contains an arsenal that promises hell a fight to remember. Eli, taking charge, instructs Hunter to show them the ammunition for the fighters.

"Time is not to be wasted," Eli declares. "It's time humans show the demons what we can do when our lives are disrupted without cause."

As they prepare for what now feels like a sacrificial mission, the fighters understand the gravity of their task.

This mission, born from grief and rage, is their stand against the evil that has plagued their world. With Josias's death as their catalyst, they are ready to deliver a reckoning hell will never forget.

***

Men, women, and children watch the battle with Berserker, their spirits ignited by the fight unfolding before them. They see Josias's plane destroyed, and one man, tears streaming from his red eyes, turns to the crowd behind him.

Arrival of Hope

"Do you see?" he yells. "People are dying for us! We cannot just stand by and let this happen!" His enthusiastic words resonate with the crowd, who feel a renewed sense of purpose and resolve.

As the man finishes his speech a demon knight lands behind him, declaring that he must be rebuked for his words against Lucifer. The demon grabs his shoulder, but the man swiftly knocks the hand away, grabs a curved knife from the demon knight's garment, and slices its neck. He then plunges the knife into the demon's forehead, killing it instantly. Standing over the fallen demon knight, he yells to the crowd, "The ultimate Armageddon has begun, but it's not for us humans. It is our destiny to protect what God has given us. If we are willing to die for it, the heavens will come to fight with us. If not, so be it."

Babylon, hearing the man's plea, sends his demon knights to conquer the crowd. However, it is too late; the humans are already armed and ready for battle. They point their weapons toward hell's army, determined to fight back with everything they have. Those without weapons pick up anything they can find, ready to engage in a battle that will last until one side has been completely obliterated.

As demon knights land and attack, blazing bullets knock them down before they can get a clear look at their attackers. On the ground, demons cut down the front line of people, but the humans fight back fiercely. Babylon, witnessing the unexpected resistance, revives his damaged head and commands all hellhounds to join the battle. He then breathes life back into Berserker, who rises with a thirst for vengeance.

Berserker, armed with his deadly double-edged axe, flies toward the crowd, blocking bullets with his powerful weapon. He chops down anyone in his path, creating a bloodbath. But more humans join the fight, picking up weapons and continuing the battle. Both sides suffer heavy losses, and the fight seems like nothing more than mutual destruction.

Arrival of Hope

However, the humans' indomitable spirit surprises the forces of hell. Babylon, seeing his demon knights struggling against the resilient humans, stands on his hind legs and lets out a deafening roar. He slams his front legs down, causing a massive earthquake that throws everyone off their feet. He then opens his mouth and breathes fire, burning everything in front of him, including his own warriors. The humans, undeterred, turn their weapons on Babylon, ready to perish rather than live under his rule.

The battle rages on, a testament to the unyielding human spirit. Despite the overwhelming odds, they fight with a ferocity that takes the forces of hell by surprise. The tide begins to turn as the humans, driven by love for their world and their kin, start to prevail.

Babylon, enraged and desperate, prepares to unleash his full fury. The humans, undaunted, brace themselves for the fight of their lives, ready to give everything to protect their beloved earth. The stage is set for a final, cataclysmic showdown between the forces of good and evil, with the fate of humanity hanging in the balance.

The scene at the Sword of Hell, where the demon knights reap blood, is a vision of pure chaos and unrelenting carnage. Humans and demon knights alike fall by the thousands, their bodies littering the battlefield as the bloodshed continues without mercy. The dragon Babylon, accompanied by his ruthless demon knight warriors, rampages through the ranks of human fighters, leaving death and destruction in his wake. Despite the overwhelming odds, the humans continue to fight with a fierce determination, fueled by the belief that God has not forsaken them, believing they are blessed.

During this carnage, both sides fight with the ferocity of wild wolves, each struggling for dominance. The ground is soaked in blood, the air filled with the sounds of clashing weapons and agonized screams. Then the very earth shakes as the entrance between earth and hell, created by Babylon, shifts from an orange sun fire to a blood-red sun fire. All eyes turn to the hellish portal as it spews forth a new wave of terror.

Arrival of Hope

From the great hole in the earth's surface, millions of new demon knights emerge, swarming like killer bees and ready to bring further death and destruction to humanity. But they are not alone. Following them is the most feared figure in all of creation, the one who strikes terror into the hearts of men and demons alike: Lucifer, the master of hell.

Lucifer's arrival halts the battle momentarily as all, even the mighty dragon Babylon, bow in fear and reverence.

The people, taking advantage of this brief respite quickly gather weapons and ammo, retreating to their hiding places to devise a plan. They know that the ceasefire will be short-lived, and they must prepare for the next onslaught.

As Lucifer strides forward, each step echoes like a drumbeat, shaking the ground with his fury. His anger is channeled at Babylon, who has shown weakness in the face of human resistance. Without a word, Lucifer commands Babylon to look him in the eye. He questions the dragon's pitiful performance and, in a display of dominance, backhands one of Babylon's heads. He then grabs another head, slamming it into the ground with a force that shakes the earth.

Babylon, beaten and cowed, retreats to a corner, hoping to avoid further punishment. But Lucifer has not finished. He leaps into the air and lands a devastating blow on Babylon's central head, causing the ground to tremble with the impact. He grabs the dragon once more, demanding an explanation for the weakness Babylon has shown.

"Why should I not kill you for this failure?" Lucifer hisses, his voice cold and unforgiving.

Babylon, knowing that any answer will be his last, remains silent, his once-mighty form now a picture of fear and submission.

In the shadows, the humans watch this display of power, their resolve hardening. They know that if they are to survive, they must be ready to fight with everything they have. The momentary ceasefire has given them a chance to regroup and rearm, but the true battle is yet to come. As Lucifer's wrath is unleashed upon Babylon, the humans prepare for the

Arrival of Hope

inevitable continuation of the war, their spirits unbroken and their determination steeled by the sight of their enemy's internal strife.

The battle for Earth is far from over, and the humans, driven by the belief that they are not forsaken, prepare to face the full fury of hell's armies once more.

Babylon, bruised and battered, speaks to Lucifer in a deep, evil voice, declaring his undying loyalty. He professes his willingness to die at Lucifer's command, expressing that it would be an honor to sacrifice his life for his master.

Lucifer, unimpressed and filled with disdain, transforms into a crystalline blue form. "For an imbecile," Lucifer sneers, "your words were well chosen, but I show no mercy." He declares his intention to destroy Babylon with his own hands. Turning his attention to his demon knights, Lucifer commands them to rise and collect the fresh blood spilled on the battlefield, intending to drink it as wine in celebration of his impending victory. He then calls the arch demon Berserker to his side to escort him to the throne Babylon had created for himself. As they enter the throne, Lucifer undergoes another transformation, this time assuming the appearance of a well-dressed man, complete with a million-dollar suit and a deceivingly human complexion.

Babylon, seething with jealousy and anger at Berserker, grows more determined to annihilate the humans who wield machines powerful enough to challenge his demon knights. Inside his throne on Earth, Lucifer asks Berserker if women have been amassed for his pleasures. Berserker assures Lucifer that all the women are waiting, ready for his pleasure. Lucifer warns Berserker against touching what belongs to him, threatening dire consequences if he disobeys. Berserker, pledging his loyalty, leads Lucifer to the waiting women.

***

Back in North Carolina, the nine soldiers finish loading the mech fighters and their ammunition, preparing to return to

Arrival of Hope

New York City. Ethan, frustrated by the limitations, asks Eli about transporting a mech tank to the battlefield. Eli dismisses the idea as impractical, but Ethan remains determined to find a way. He heads to the weapons warehouse to devise a solution for transporting the heavy tank to New York.

Charlie, overwhelmed by memories of Josias' death, returns to the control room and surveys the battlefield through a satellite feed. He is awestruck to see the demon knights, including Babylon, standing still as if paralyzed by fear. Moving the camera, he spots Lucifer's throne and realizes the devil himself has arrived. Panicking, Charlie rushes to warn the others, understanding that they face an even greater threat than before.

As Charlie alerts the group, Hunter joins him, and they both recognize the dire situation. The soldiers and their allies prepare for a final stand, knowing the next battle will be the most challenging yet.

***

In New York City the humans lay in wait, armed with advanced weapons and explosives, ready to unleash a coordinated attack.

At the signal, hundreds of explosives are hurled from the buildings, creating a devastating series of blasts. Flames and shrapnel engulf the demon knights below, and even Babylon is forced to shield himself with his wings.

The humans, undeterred by the inferno, surge forward, shooting anything that moves. Those armed with missile launchers take strategic positions, targeting the demon knights from above.

Lucifer, enraged by the assault, emerges from his throne alongside Berserker. He witnesses the annihilation of his demon warriors and acknowledges the humans' determination. Berserker flies off to fulfill Lucifer's command to decapitate any armed human. However, a well-

Arrival of Hope

aimed missile strikes Lucifer in the chest. As the smoke clears, Lucifer remains unscathed, his eyes glowing with fury. He retaliates by launching a glowing blue sphere, obliterating the building from which the missile has been launched.

At Lucifer's command, Babylon and the demon knights resume their massacre. Despite the humans' valiant efforts, they face overwhelming odds. Lucifer, finding little challenge in the humans' resistance, joins his army in the slaughter.

High above the earth, in the celestial realms, a son asks his father if the time has come. The father, surrounded by other celestial beings, replies that the seventh has not yet called. "When he calls, the time will be," he says. "Until then, we watch and wait."

In the heavens, a sense of anticipation hangs in the air as the battle below rages on, both sides locked in a deadly struggle for the fate of the earth.

***

At the North Carolina airport, the mech and stealth fighters are readying for departure. Eight fighters will head to New York City, leaving Charlie behind to control the satellites from the Oblivion System, which could be crucial in saving their lives. The airport lights illuminate the runway for a perfect liftoff. Ethan, ecstatic he has managed to secure the tank, uses piles of bungee cords and chains to attach it to three mech fighters piloted by Biggs, James, and Eli. He instructs them to take off slowly to ensure the cords and chains stretch without tearing the fighters apart.

Charlie, already feeling the isolation of having been left behind, checks the lines connected to the tank one last time. He then signals the three fighters to take to the dark, bloody skies. The engines of the mech fighters roar to life simultaneously as they roll down the runway, dragging the tank behind them. As they lift off at the runway's end, the tank ascends slowly into the air. Seeing the successful takeoff, the remaining fighters start their engines one by one, speeding into the night sky, driven by a fierce desire for vengeance.

Charlie rushes back inside the airport, heading to the control room. He turns off all the lights, sits at the main controls, and begins weaving the satellites toward the battle-ravaged New York City. Through the satellite feeds, he witnesses the ongoing battle as people make their final stand, ready to sacrifice everything. Charlie updates the eight mech fighters on the situation, emphasizing the need to watch out for Lucifer, the Devil. He vows to support the people on the ground, providing them with more hope and firepower.

Eli acknowledges Charlie's plan, encouraging him to do whatever is necessary to secure victory. Charlie powers up the Oblivion satellites, gradually increasing their power until they are fully operational. He targets clusters of demon knights, firing with a fervent passion to reclaim Earth for humanity. As the Oblivion satellites unleash their energy, the dark skies above the battlefield begin to brighten, as if the sun is piercing through the darkness.

On the ground, the source of this newfound light is revealed to be small meteors falling from the sky, a sight that sends shivers down Berserker's spine as he recalls his last encounter with Oblivion satellites. Berserker scrambles for cover while Lucifer, perplexed, wonders what could be directing this divine power. The people below, witnessing the energy spheres striking down demon knights with precision, feel as if the heavens have joined their fight. This celestial intervention boosts their morale, filling them with renewed courage and hope.

As the battle rages on, humans, demons, and hellhounds clash fiercely, each side determined to emerge victorious. The people of Earth, who had once bowed down in despair, now stand tall, emboldened by the divine intervention and strength provided by their eternal creator. The mech stealth fighters, the chosen defenders of humanity, ready themselves for the ultimate sacrifice, knowing their actions could turn the tide of this celestial war.

Every moment is critical as they brace for the impending chaos. The battle is far from over, and the resolve of the humans to reclaim their world from the clutches of hell burns brighter than ever. The intervention from above, coupled with the unyielding spirit of humanity, creates a glimmer of hope in the midst of their darkest hour. The final confrontation is imminent and all eyes are on the battlefield, waiting to see if Earth can rise from the ashes of its destruction.

In the cacophony of death on the ground, the noise of approaching flying machines pierces the air, matching the demonic shrieks. These machines are a nuisance to Babylon, saviors to the people, but insignificant to Lucifer, the great devil. The eight fighters make a sweeping turn, directing their focus on the dragon Babylon. Eli instructs the three fighters to hurry and land the tank, referring to it as the "hunk of steel," so they can join the grim task of engaging the dragon. The three fighters dive toward an open space, land the tank, release the heavy artillery, and swiftly return to the sky, rejoining the others in the fierce battle against Babylon and his minions. Forming a battle formation, they unleash their armaments at Babylon. Eli commands them to break off and attack from all sides, hoping to flip the dragon and expose his vulnerable underside. The initial missiles are nullified by Babylon's massive wings, but they serve as a diversion. A stealth mech sneaks into position, giving Babylon no time to react.

Stealth fighters catch Babylon with direct hits from all sides, shocking but not defeating him. They circle around, firing armor-piercing homing bullets, which only irritate the dragon. Babylon grows angrier, his power surging. Meanwhile Lucifer, crushing the throats of two men and impaling another with his right leg, stares skyward, mesmerized by the machines challenging his forces.

Arrival of Hope

Ethan notices fewer ground shots, suggesting to the fighters that it is time to drop more ammunition on the ground forces. He breaks off, diving toward a crowd of people, blasting demon knights as he descends, providing hope for the beleaguered humans. Charlie tracks Ethan's movements, clearing a path with the satellites. Lucifer, observing the protection Ethan receives, unleashes a dark red ray, striking Ethan's plane. Though damaged, Ethan drops a crate of weapons and returns to the battle, ignoring his compromised fighter.

Caught off guard, Ethan is damaged by Babylon's flames, sending his mech spiraling back to the ground. He ejects just in time, parachuting toward the tank. As he descends demon knights close in, but Ethan, armed with his specialized AR-15, picks them off with precision. Landing amidst the chaos, Ethan directs the people to the tank, suggesting they start it to target Lucifer's throne.

One man mentions women captured inside the throne, prompting Ethan to agree on a rescue attempt. They move swiftly toward the tank, planting explosives along the way. The stealth fighters continue their assault on Babylon, aided by Charlie's satellite beams. This coordinated attack finally brings the dragon down.

Lucifer, enraged by Babylon's defeat, undergoes a terrifying transformation. His body glows purple, energy surging around him, tearing the environment apart. He morphs into a colossal demon ruler with circular horns, black eyes, bull-like feet, lion's teeth, three-fingered hands, and bat-eagle wings. His dark, bloody red complexion has streaks of pulsating purple lines. Now towering over fifteen feet tall, Lucifer surveys the battlefield, deciding which mech fighter will be the first to feel his wrath.

Lucifer's gaze locks onto a fearless approaching fighter. The fighter fires at Lucifer, unaware of the doom awaiting. With a mighty roar, Lucifer lunges, preparing to obliterate his adversary in a display of demonic power.

Arrival of Hope

The pulsating power around Lucifer surges intensely, flowing back into his body, filling his eyes, mouth, and leaking through the purple stripes permanently etched on his skin. As his power clears, Lucifer channels energy into his right hand, raises it toward the sky, and conjures violet lightning. He strikes the first mech fighter fiercely, then follows with a second strike from the dark sky, sending the mech spiraling out of control toward the tank's location.

Gage, witnessing this, is drawn to the fallen fighter, trying to contact the stealth units, but there is no response—too close to the ground. He watches helplessly as the fighter crashes near the tank, engulfed in an explosion with no survivors, including his brother, Mike. For a moment Gage closes his eyes, mourning the loss. Then he reopens them, focusing on Lucifer for the last battle. Gage and the remaining fighters release their weapons for the people below, then prepare for their last stand against Lucifer.

As they drop the weapon crates, a signal inside their mechs starts blinking out of ammo. Realizing the mechs are now useless, they all aim their mechs at Lucifer, ejecting just before impact. The mechs, intended as a distraction, aim to crash into Lucifer. However, Lucifer erects an energy field, blocking the mechs and explosions and keeping himself unharmed.

Meanwhile, the six remaining fighters are busy dodging demon knights. Charlie provides cover from the sky, using a powerful military weapon left behind at the airport. Suddenly, a demon knight appears in front of Adonis, surprising him and giving him no time to react. As the demon prepares to strike, a loud noise from the ground distracts it, causing it to turn and inadvertently tear Adonis' parachute.

An object from the ground speeds toward the demon knight, splitting it in half. Adonis releases himself from the damaged parachute, falling helplessly but aiming for a pile of dead bodies to cushion his fall. He lands hard but manages to get to his feet quickly, grabbing his rifle and rejoining the battle. The other fighters, seeing Adonis' maneuver, follow suit, landing with minimal injury. They attribute their survival to the power of God, though they remain uncertain.

As the war rages on, a voice from heaven speaks. A divine presence rises, telling his son it is time for the gathering of the chosen ones. The final confrontation with Lucifer is imminent, and the fighters, armed with newfound hope and divine intervention, prepare for their ultimate showdown. The son of the one who has just spoken, the divine messenger, places his hands together as if in prayer, bows his head, closes his eyes, and, with a thought, disappears from heaven, smiling in joy but with a serious demeanor.

He reappears on Earth, surrounded by the vast waters of the Atlantic Ocean near the crash site of the warrior named Josias. Walking along the ocean floor as if it were dry land, a radiant light envelops him, illuminating the dark depths. As he moves the dead fish come back to life and pollution is miraculously cleansed, infusing the ocean with renewed vitality. The sea creatures, recognizing the divine presence, swim away or hide, knowing this man as the Son of the living God, a member of the Celestial Council.

Upon reaching the wreckage where Josias lies lifeless, the Son raises his right arm, clearing the debris. He looks at Josias' body and, with an open hand, grants him sight.

Josias awakens in a panic, bewildered by the surrounding water, but soon realizes he is not drowning. He sees a radiant figure before him and, without opening his mouth, mentally asks, "Who are you?"

The Son of God responds clearly, "I am the Son of the living God, sent to guide you against the forces of hell. You are the sixth warrior, chosen to wield the sixth star and staff of the new revelation."

Josias, still confused, asks, "Why me?"

The Son of God replies, "You have believed in the heavens and held no ties to the lies spoken by others. Your faith in humanity and the divine has never wavered. You accepted your fate, and now you are blessed by the power of the living

Arrival of Hope

God and the Celestial Council. You are the sixth warrior, a hybrid tasked with helping to eliminate the forces of hell."

The Son raises his right arm, opening his hand to reveal a star that resembles the universe. He hands it to Josias, saying, "Your quest is to bring hell to its knees, restoring Earth and humanity to their true glory. For they all shall become like you."

As Josias accepts the star, it absorbs into his body, initiating a profound transformation. He grows rapidly, breaking free from the restraints of his seat. Standing tall, Josias declares, "I will not fail this heavenly mission."

The Son of God then vanishes, moving swiftly to find the seventh and final warrior, the one destined to hold the final star and staff of heaven.

With Josias now empowered and ready to join the battle, the tides of war on Earth shift as the chosen warriors prepare to confront the forces of hell, bringing hope to humanity in its darkest hour.

Josias watches as the Son of the living God departs in an instant, then looks up toward the surface of the ocean.

With newfound strength and determination, he soars from the depths, his wings spreading wide, their colors a crystalline-blue moonlight adorned with spots resembling the universe and bright stars. As he ascends, Josias makes his way back to the war-torn landscape of New York City where humanity's fate hangs in the balance.

Simultaneously, the Son of God, whose name remains unknown, continues his divine mission, seeking the next chosen one destined to wield the seventh star of heaven.

His journey brings him to the site where Mike, the brother of Gage, lies in the middle of the chaotic battlefield. With a wave of his hand, the Son of God clears the wreckage surrounding Mike's lifeless body and restores him to life.

Mike awakens to a surreal and serene darkness filled with bright, star-like essences. The presence of the heavenly figure before him compels Mike to fall to his knees in awe, feeling a profound sense of peace.

Arrival of Hope

The Son of God gently encourages Mike to rise, instructing him to worship only the almighty God. He explains that they are all children of the Heavenly Father, destined to serve Him. Mike stands, ready to receive his divine gift.

The Son of God raises his right hand, presenting Mike with a small, brilliant star shaped like a universe. Tears of joy stream down Mike's face as he grasps the star, feeling an overwhelming sense of heavenly mercy and a renewed purpose.

The star merges with Mike's body, transforming him into a celestial hybrid, ready to join Josias and the other chosen warriors in their sacred mission. As the transformation completes, the Son of God smiles, then fades away, dissolving into the essence of the air. Before disappearing completely, he eliminates the immediate threats surrounding Mike, ensuring his safety.

Mike, now empowered, spreads his arms wide and looks up at the dark, bleeding sky. He releases a radiant burst of heavenly energy, drawing the attention of everyone on the battlefield, including Lucifer. The powerful display signifies a turning point in the battle. Lucifer, recognizing that his plans for domination are slipping away, shifts his focus. His new goal is to obliterate all life on Earth, ensuring no future generations can be born to reclaim and rebuild the world.

The forces of good and evil converge in a climactic showdown. Josias and Mike, the newly transformed warriors, join the fray, their combined might a beacon of hope for the embattled humans. With the power of the celestial stars within them, they fight to drive back the demonic invaders and reclaim Earth for humanity. The war rages on, but now with divine intervention and the rise of the chosen warriors, the tide begins to turn in favor of those who fight for light and life.

As Mike soars through the air a familiar figure rejoins him, a fellow hybrid, Josias. They exchange a quick glance and simultaneously exclaim, "Cool! Nice to see you again." Their camaraderie is palpable, a beacon of hope amid the chaos.

Arrival of Hope

Other fighters notice the hybrids in the sky, but their identities remain a mystery to them.

Meanwhile, Berserker and another arch demon knight named Wraith attempt to ambush the warrior angels. However, Mike and Josias sense their presence and swiftly turn, grabbing both arch demon knights by the throats. Mike seizes Wraith, while Josias captures Berserker.

Mike accelerates toward the ground, dragging Wraith with him. They crash through the concrete, landing in a sewer below. Mike's newfound abilities make him an unstoppable force. With his left hand still gripping Wraith's throat, Mike uses his right hand to punch through Wraith's chest, extracting and crushing his green heart. Wraith's life ends instantly, with Mike showing no hesitation, pity, or regrets. He is resolute in his mission to cleanse Earth of the hellish invaders. Josias, still holding Berserker by the throat, brings their faces close. Josias asks if Berserker remembers him, and as Berserker's eyes widen in recognition, Josias confirms his identity with a sinister grin. "By the hand of the living, it is the one who remembers, who you remember, And now the one who will destroy you from the thoughts of all who see you."

Josias's eyes begin to glow a bright blue, radiating pure angelic power. Despite Berserker's struggles, Josias's grip remains unbreakable. Josias releases two powerful beams from his eyes, burning through Berserker's forehead and exiting the back of his head without spilling a drop of his evil green blood. Josias then hoists Berserker's lifeless body into the air and hurls it toward Lucifer, the body landing at Lucifer's feet.

The hybrids, Mike and Josias, now stand side by side, ready to confront Lucifer. But before they can strike Lucifer vanishes in an instant, reappearing beside the lifeless body of the dragon Babylon. The battlefield has ignited with tension as the hybrids, and the forces of hell prepare for the next phase of their epic confrontation.

Arrival of Hope

The two hybrids, Mike and Josias, stand side by side, their focus shifting from Lucifer to the chaos of the battle below. Their mission is clear: eliminate the demon knights that have gained the upper hand over the human fighters.

***

Meanwhile, Ethan and his team inside the tank are determined to breach Lucifer's throne, rescue the captured women, and destroy the facility of evil.

The mech tank rumbles up the steps of the throne, crashing through the walls with a resounding impact. Five rebels, including Ethan, exit the tank and spread out to plant explosives, each equipped with a detonator. Ethan issues a stern reminder: they have ten minutes to return to the tank, or they will be presumed dead, and the throne will be shattered to pieces.

The throne is eerily empty due to the ongoing battle outside. One of the rebels, his nerves frayed, creeps down a long, deserted hallway. Every little sound makes him jump, his finger twitching on the trigger. He catches sight of a shadow darting from one room to another, leading him to follow, albeit warily.

Inside the room, he finds three naked women on a round bed with red silk sheets, moaning and touching each other as if oblivious to the war raging outside. They are now part of hell's family, transformed into Lucifer's servants.

The sight puts the man, a sage before Babylon's wings spread the fires from below, in a trance, his sexual urges overriding his sense of duty. He drops his gun, sheds his shirt, and approaches the bed, succumbing to seduction.

As the women begin to caress him, his fantasies take over. One woman engages him intimately while another kisses him, and the third watches, rubbing his chest. But the situation quickly turns horrific. The woman's face morphs into a demonic visage, and she bites off his penis, spitting it out before they all pounce on him like ravenous wolves. His

Arrival of Hope

screams echo through the halls, drawing the attention of others including Ethan who is searching for survivors.

By the time Ethan and the others arrive, it is too late. They find the man's mutilated body, his legs gone, one arm missing, and a gaping hole in his chest The Mungai, the spiritual leader who has rebelled against fearing the demonic forces mutters that the man has been foolish to think he can fight against the minions of Babylon, celestial or physical only to fall into the seduction of pleasure, but Ethan responds somberly, "No one deserves to perish like this, no matter their mistakes."

Ethan closes the man's remaining eye, and the group surveys the empty room, the demonic women nowhere to be seen. Another rebel asks if Ethan knows what could have done this. Ethan speculates, "Maybe hellhounds, those damned dogs of hell."

Unaware that the women are responsible, they collect the fallen man's rifle and continue their grim search for the captured women. The air is thick with tension and the smell of blood, the reality of their perilous mission sinking in with every step. They move cautiously, ready to confront whatever horrors Lucifer's throne has in store for them.

Ethan, the last to leave the room, looks up at the entrance doorway before exiting and sees the man's legs hanging from the ceiling, strangely bloodless. This sight cements his suspicions: they are not dealing with Hellhounds. Realizing they are not alone, he turns to the others, who have just regrouped.

One of the men voices what everyone is thinking: "We need to stick together. This splitting up is suicide. We're stronger as a unit." Ethan agrees, as do the others. They move as one, planting explosives in strategic locations as they go, ensuring that if they do not return the throne will still be destroyed.

***

Outside, Lucifer has his own dark plans.

Arrival of Hope

Standing at the head of the lifeless body of the dragon
Babylon, he summons the evil star of death into his left hand.
This star, red and dull, seems to drip with blood and screams
as if souls were trapped within. Holding the star over one of
Babylon's heads, Lucifer intones a dark incantation. "Behold
what I have planted inside you, my pet. This is a star holding
a dead universe, one which you destroyed yourself millennia
ago. Inside this star is the power of a red sun, a dead sun."
As Lucifer speaks Babylon's body begins to glow with a
bright red light, bleeding energy into the surrounding area.
"I bring your life from this star, this dead thing. I bring you
seven lives, for you will no longer be one. You will be seven,
separated to scatter your massacre of total destruction, for I
have commanded it, your king, your master, your lord, the
devil Lucifer."
With Lucifer's final words, a red sphere of evil energy
surrounds them, securing Babylon's transformation. The air
is consumed with the sounds of roaring, yelling, and laughter
from within the sphere. The angelic hybrids, Mike and Josias,
see the transformation taking place. Without hesitation they
try to penetrate the sphere but are repelled by its dark energy.

***

In heaven, God addresses the Celestial Council. "It is time to
send the remaining angels to join Mike and Josias." The Son
looks down toward the earth, and with a wave of his right
arm he parts the dark clouds, commanding the last five angels
to descend to Earth to fight alongside the hybrids.
As the protective sphere around Lucifer and Babylon
dissolves into thin air, it reveals seven smaller dragons, each
half the size of Babylon but just as lethal. These dragons,
each named Babylon, symbolized a new era of destruction.
Mike and Josias clench their fists, filled with righteous fury.
They prepare to battle the new dragons when the sky above
them opens, revealing the separation of the dark, bloody

Arrival of Hope

clouds. At first they think it is more demon knights, readying themselves for another onslaught.

But instead five angels descend from the heavens, their radiant forms contrasting starkly against the dark backdrop of the war-torn sky. The hybrids know then that they are not alone in this fight. The celestial reinforcements bring new hope.

The combined forces of heaven and earth gather their strength. Mike and Josias, flanked by the newly arrived angels, face the seven new dragons. The angels' divine light illuminates the battlefield, instilling courage in the hearts of the human fighters below.

The battle is far from over, but with the hybrids and angels united, there is a renewed sense of determination to drive out the evil that has plagued their world. With a shared nod, Mike and Josias lead the charge, their hearts burning with the will to protect their planet and its people from the forces of hell.

The five angels, now fully revealed, unleash their heavenly powers toward the seven dragons, as well as a barrage toward Lucifer himself. Descending to Earth, they form a straight line across the dark, bloody skies, hovering side by side with Josias and Mike. The radiant, sun-like rays of their heavenly auras fill the area, casting a divine light that makes Lucifer cringe in disgust. Furious, Lucifer commands the seven dragons to attack, promising them the heads of the angels and hybrids as their reward for a feast.

The seven celestial beings—angels and hybrids alike—engage the dragons, each choosing their target. The dark sky becomes a battleground, with the forces of good and evil clashing violently. Below, Charlie continues his vigil from North Carolina, directing his weapon fire toward the demons infesting New York City. Zooming in on the battle, Charlie's cameras capture the faces of the seven angelic beings. Recognizing Josias among them, Charlie is momentarily lost in disbelief. He sees Josias evade a flame attack from one of

Arrival of Hope

the dragons, turning to face the camera. Josias smiles and salutes Charlie, signaling him to head to New York City. Startled and excited, Charlie knocks over two buckets of water in his rush, shorting out the computer systems and causing a small explosion that dazes him. Determined, Charlie grabs his M16 rifle and leaves the control room, heading to the last mech fighter to join the battle in New York City.

***

Back at Lucifer's throne, Ethan and his men continue their search for the captured women. The throne trembles from the external battle's intensity. Pausing to listen, they hear faint but distinct female voices. Following the sounds, they find themselves at a dead-end wall. Upon pressing their ears to the wall, they can confirm that the women are behind it.
After a strenuous effort they manage to push the wall open, revealing the women tied to the ceiling by their wrists, naked and distraught.
Cautious and skeptical, Ethan and his team approach slowly. Before they can free the women three other ladies burst into the room, warning them not to release the captives. The newcomers claimed they have been hiding and that the hanging women are demons in disguise, meant to entrap and entice rescuers.
Despite the warnings, one of Ethan's men starts to release a woman. As soon as she is free she puts him in a sexual trance before brutally killing him. The hanging women transform into full-blown demons, ready to devour their prey. The three newcomers reiterate their warning with a sarcastic "I told you so" and urge Ethan and his men to follow them. Realizing the gravity of the situation, Ethan and his team flee, hoping they are not running into another trap.
Outside, the seven dragons, now unleashed, wreak havoc. Josias and Mike, alongside the five angels, fight valiantly, their divine powers clashing with the dragons' infernal might.

Arrival of Hope

While there is chaos, the celestial reinforcements provide a beacon of hope, rallying the human fighters below.
As the battle rages on, the combined forces of heaven and earth stand united against the tide of hellish invaders.
Ethan, leading his team through the maze of Lucifer's throne, clings to the hope that their efforts turn the tide. Meanwhile, Charlie's imminent arrival in New York City brings renewed determination, knowing that the fight for Earth's salvation is far from over. With every blow struck and every life saved, the resolve of the warriors of heaven and earth grows stronger, determined to reclaim their world from the clutches of darkness.
As they run down a long hallway the demon women give chase, crawling on the walls, ceiling, and floor, jostling each other to be the first to claim their prey. The men, along with the two women, quickly turn a corner, with the demon women hot on their heels. However, when the demons reach the corner they find the hallway empty.
Confused and frustrated, they continue their search.
Moments later Ethan's head emerges from the wall, where he and his companions had hidden behind an illusion. He signals to the others that the coast is clear. They all come out of hiding and hastily proceed.
Upon reaching the final corner, they find themselves in a lobby-like area near the exit of Lucifer's throne. To their horror, the demon women are already there, hanging from the ceiling and standing on the floor, drooling with anticipation. The group has no choice but to run again.

***

Meanwhile, at the North Carolina airport, Charlie is preparing to head to New York City. As he rushes toward the stealth mech fighter, he notices a line of fiery hellhounds two blocks long, ready to attack the airport.
Realizing he will not make it to the mech in time, Charlie devises a plan to deal with the hellhounds. He races toward a

Arrival of Hope

facility where water is leaking from broken pipes, hoping to use it against the fiery creatures.

The hellhounds, like a wave of fireballs, incinerate everything in their path. Charlie, feeling the heat on his heels, sprints up the stairs to the floor where the water is leaking. He knows he has only one chance to survive.

Reaching the water just in time, he positions himself under the gushing pipe, drenching himself as the hellhounds close in. The water repels the hellhounds, turning them into piles of dust and bones.

Realizing he needs to reach his mech fighter, Charlie picks up a piece of broken pipe, using it to redirect the water toward the hellhounds, creating an opening. Seizing the moment, he makes a dash for a broken window. Despite the hellhounds chasing him, they are unable to pass through the window, blocked by an unseen force. Exhausted but relieved, Charlie realizes he might have been saved by divine intervention. He hears a voice in his head urging him to leave immediately.

Following the mysterious advice, Charlie sprints to the mech fighter, quickly starting its engines and setting a course for New York City. As he prepares for takeoff, he sees a massive tidal wave hovering in the sky, held in place. The voice in his head tells him to fly through the water. Trusting the guidance, Charlie accelerates, flying through the tidal wave without incident. The wave crashes down behind him, flooding the airport and wiping out any remaining evils.

***

Back at Lucifer's throne, Ethan and his team, along with the three women, run for their lives. As they dash through the throne's dark corridors, the demonic women continue their relentless pursuit. The group reaches a dead end, with the demon women closing in fast. The three women with Ethan shout for everyone to push against the wall, revealing another hidden passage. They all scramble through just as the demon women reach them, slamming the passage shut behind them. In the skies above New York City, the battle between the celestial beings and the dragons rages on. The angels and hybrids fight valiantly, their heavenly powers clashing with the demonic fury of the dragons. The outcome of the battle remains uncertain, as both sides fight with unyielding ferocity for the fate of humanity and the world.

The battle intensifies, with each side pushing their limits. Lucifer, watching the clash from below, grits his teeth in anger as he sees the celestial beings holding their ground. He summons more demonic forces to bolster the dragons, determined to overwhelm the forces of good.

***

Charlie, now airborne, speeds toward New York City, ready to join the fight. His journey is fraught with danger, but his resolve is unshakable. As he nears the city, he sees the epic battle in the skies and knows he must do everything in his power to aid his friends and save humanity from the brink of annihilation.

***

Back at Lucifer's throne, Ethan and his team have no choice but to retreat, avoiding the demon women. As they dash down the long, demonic hallway, one of the women in the group becomes fed up with running. She grabs a rifle from one of the men and unleashes a barrage of armor-piercing bullets at the demon women. The man protests, but Ethan intervenes, telling him to let her keep the gun and handing him another rifle.

The group forms a firing line, unleashing a hail of bullets at the demon women. The possessed women, however, use telekinetic powers to create shields, deflecting the bullets, though a few manage to penetrate. Amidst the chaos, Ethan's voice booms, ordering everyone to fall back as the demon women create an invisible wall that ricochets the bullets back at them.

The team retreats, two people struck down as the rest survive the deflection, following Ethan to the area where he planted the C4 explosives. As they pass the explosives, Ethan instructs them to find cover. One of the men, in response to the women's curious looks, says with excitement, "You'll see," and tells them to get down.

Ethan stands in the open, drawing the attention of the demon women. One of them mocks him, declaring that his sacrifice is futile and that they will soon find and kill the rest. Ethan, showing no fear, prays for forgiveness and detonates the explosives. The powerful blast obliterates the demon women, blows a hole through the walls of the throne, and catches the attention of the demon knights outside.

As the dust settles, the team emerges from their hiding spots, cautiously walking through the smoke and debris.

They find parts of the demon women's bodies scattered everywhere but see no sign of Ethan. Suddenly, one of the women spots something through the clearing smoke and shouts, "Look over there!"

They see Ethan on his knees, rifle in hand, staring at the cracked ground as if in a trance. The group approaches him, bewildered at how he survived the explosion. When one of the women tries to touch him, her hand is stopped by an invisible field. Ethan rises to his feet, explaining that he believes a celestial being or God created the protective field. Apologizing for scaring them, Ethan leads the group to the blown wall, ready to exit the throne. They board a nearby tank and drive away. Once they are at a safe distance, Ethan detonates the remaining explosives, collapsing Lucifer's throne and sending a powerful message to hell: leave or be obliterated.

The destruction of the throne reverberates across the battlefield. The celestial forces and hybrids battling in the skies above New York City feel a surge of hope, while

Arrival of Hope

Lucifer and his minions have become momentarily thrown into disarray. Ethan's sacrifice and miraculous survival become a beacon of resilience and defiance against the forces of darkness.

Back in the dark, blood-soaked skies of New York City, the battle rages on. The streets run red with the blood of the fallen, both good and evil, as Lucifer revels in the carnage. His hunger for the ugliest deaths is insatiable, even consuming his own demonic forces. Amidst this chaos, the seven dragons unleash their fury, targeting the five angels, two hybrids sent by God, and the celestial beings.

Josias, the sixth warrior angel and hybrid, grows weary after four days of continuous battle. He raises his right hand toward the sky, clenching his fingers and drawing forth lightning and meteor-like spheres from the blood-red clouds. He hurls these at the dragon he is fighting, reducing it to a pile of bones and dust. Awed by his own power, Josias proclaims the might of the heavens.

Meanwhile, Mike, the seventh warrior angel hybrid, is pinned down by another dragon head, enduring a torrent of hellfire. Despite the searing pain, Mike shows no fear. His eyes blaze as bright as the sun, releasing a powerful light that pierces the dragon's chest. The dragon's screams echo with the agony of cursed souls, and it disintegrates into a mass of worms and maggots.

As Josias and Mike turn their attention to Lucifer, the other five warrior angels continue their battle against the remaining dragons. Each side exchanges fierce blows, but the angels' divine strength prevails. One by one, the dragons fall, their defeat marked by the heavenly power wielded by the angels. As the battle rages on, one angel finds himself in a crisis, facing the last dragon alone. Accepting his fate, the angel delivers a prophecy, declaring the dragon's doom. Just as the dragon prepares to incinerate him, a series of fiery streaks strike the dragon from the sky. The angel looks up to see a mech fighter, piloted by Charlie, providing unexpected assistance. Together, they obliterate the dragon.

Arrival of Hope

Charlie ejects from his damaged mech, landing amidst the bloodbath on the ground. He fights fiercely, quickly joined by a crowd of warriors, including his brother, Hunter. With the dragons defeated, the focus shifts to Lucifer, who has become enraged by the failure of his forces. Holding the mutilated remains of a man and a woman, he taunts the seven angels and hybrids now surrounding him.

Decius, one of the angels, calls out to Lucifer, demanding his surrender. Lucifer, licking the blood from his fingers, mocks them and vows to turn their heads into ornaments for his throne. Michael, revealed as the first angel and Lucifer's brother, retorts that the earth will once again devour him. Lucifer responds by creating a small earthquake and hurling its energy at the angels, knocking them back. He then transforms into a fearsome demon resembling a leopard with a bear's feet and a lion's mouth. The transformation shocks the surrounding humans, but not the angels.

The seven angels and hybrids counterattack with their divine powers, overwhelming Lucifer and bringing him to his knees. However, Lucifer rises again, deflecting their combined forces back at them and knocking them down.

The final confrontation is at hand, as the angels and hybrids prepare for their ultimate battle against the Prince of Darkness.

The devil, Satan, ascends into the sky, unleashing torrents of evil rays and dark mystical powers upon the seven angelic beings below. He taunts them with threats of drinking their holy blood alongside that of the humans, basking in the satisfaction of their destruction. The battle rages on for hours and days, with the angels and hybrids appearing to be on the losing side. Lucifer absorbs the divine energy emanating from their immortal bodies, and he is on the brink of victory. The seven angelic beings, exhausted and defeated, lie on their backs as Lucifer stands over them, declaring his victory. The fighting ceases, and a hush falls over the battlefield as everyone, both humans and demon knights, witness the apparent fall of heaven's warriors. Lucifer, in his moment of triumph, turns his attention to the spectators, proclaiming his dominance. He does not notice the angels are still alive, silently invoking the power of the kingdom of heaven and the Son who has granted them the strength to protect Earth.

As the angels' cries echo across the planet, the dark, bloody skies begin to part. Realizing the impending divine intervention, Lucifer attempts to stop it but finds himself powerless. A section of the sky brightens, revealing a celestial army of angelic beings descending. Desperate, Lucifer and his demon knights turn on the humans for a final attempt at destruction. However, the heavens respond swiftly. Millions of angels, their bodies glowing like the universe, descend upon the battlefield. Two angels land on each demon knight, obliterating their flesh and souls, leaving no trace of their evil behind.

Within hours, Lucifer is alone, surrounded by the victorious angels. Captured and awaiting the presence of God, he stands defiant. The darkness still shrouds the earth, but the arrival of the heavenly host brings hope and light to the eyes of every human. A beam of light descends from the sky, heralding the arrival of God and His Son. The celestial beings land before Lucifer, declaring his judgment.

Lucifer, laughing menacingly, claims he cannot die. God and His Son manifest in solid form, with God speaking of Lucifer's impending punishment. Commanded to rise, Lucifer prepares for battle, unleashing his full power in a blinding explosion. The blast, contained within a circle of angels, seems catastrophic, but the power of the heavens prevails. As the smoke clears, it becomes evident that Lucifer's efforts were in vain.

Falling to his knees, Lucifer pleads for mercy, but none is given. God crosses His arms and delivers the final judgment, condemning Lucifer to a fate worse than death.

Covered in divine wrath, Lucifer's screams fill the air until he is reduced to a mere mortal, suffering the same fate he inflicted upon others. God then douses the great tunnel of

Arrival of Hope

fire, releasing the lost souls and eradicating the hell Lucifer created.

With the words "let there be light," the sky clears, revealing a bright sun and a cloudless sky. Humanity rejoices, basking in the warmth and light they have long been deprived of. The Son of God calls forth the brave individuals who fought valiantly—Eli, James, Biggs, Gage, Hunter, Charlie, Adonis, Ethan, Josias, Mike, and the three courageous women. Each kneels before God and is granted the ability to traverse between heaven and earth at will.

God addresses all of humanity, proclaiming Himself the Alpha and Omega, offering the fountain of life to those who thirst and promising that those who overcome shall inherit all things. He instructs them to repair the earth with love, without seeking profit, and to live in harmony, exploring the universe, as it has always been their gift.

The earth, now a place of peace and goodness, becomes a beacon of light in the universe. God speaks to His other children across the cosmos, announcing that humanity has awakened and will now be the bearers of light and justice. They will comfort each other and destroy evil, spreading the vibrations of the heavens and demonstrating the true power of the divine. With Josias and Mike as the first to give rise to the indomitable human spirit, humanity steps into its true role, ready to guide and protect the universe under the watchful eyes of the heavens.

Author - Josias Mibzstarus